stuck WITH YOU

AN ENEMIES TO LOVERS ROMANCE

MONI BOYCE

Cover Design ©Bailey Cover Boutique
Formatting: Aubree Valentine with Forever Write PR
Editing: Duli Noted
Proofreading: Yvette Deon
Managed by: Forever Write PR

Kindle ISBN Number: 978-1-952691-91-1
PRINT ISBN Number: 978-1-952691-01-0

BLURB

Can enemies turn into lovers over the course of a week?

Maddie

When I decided to attend my high school reunion, I knew I'd run the risk of running into Jack Carter. Mr. Big Time Country Music Star. The same guy that broke my heart in high school. What I didn't expect was that the resort would mess up our reservations, and we'd end up roommates.

Now I'm stuck sharing a cabin with him for the next week, and I don't know whether I want to kill him or kiss him.

Jack

What are the odds I would end up sharing a cabin with my ex-high school sweetheart, Maddie Grace? The woman was a sweet tomboy back then, now she's a knockout, uptight lawyer, who loves to argue. Even though we fight like cats and dogs, I'm feeling that familiar old spark and the more time I spend with her, the more I'm beginning to think letting her go was my biggest mistake.

Thanks to a little mix-up at the resort, I've now got a week to prove to her that we belong together and you can bet I'm going to give it my best shot.

Escape to the romantic paradise of Holiday Springs and warm up with your next happily ever after.

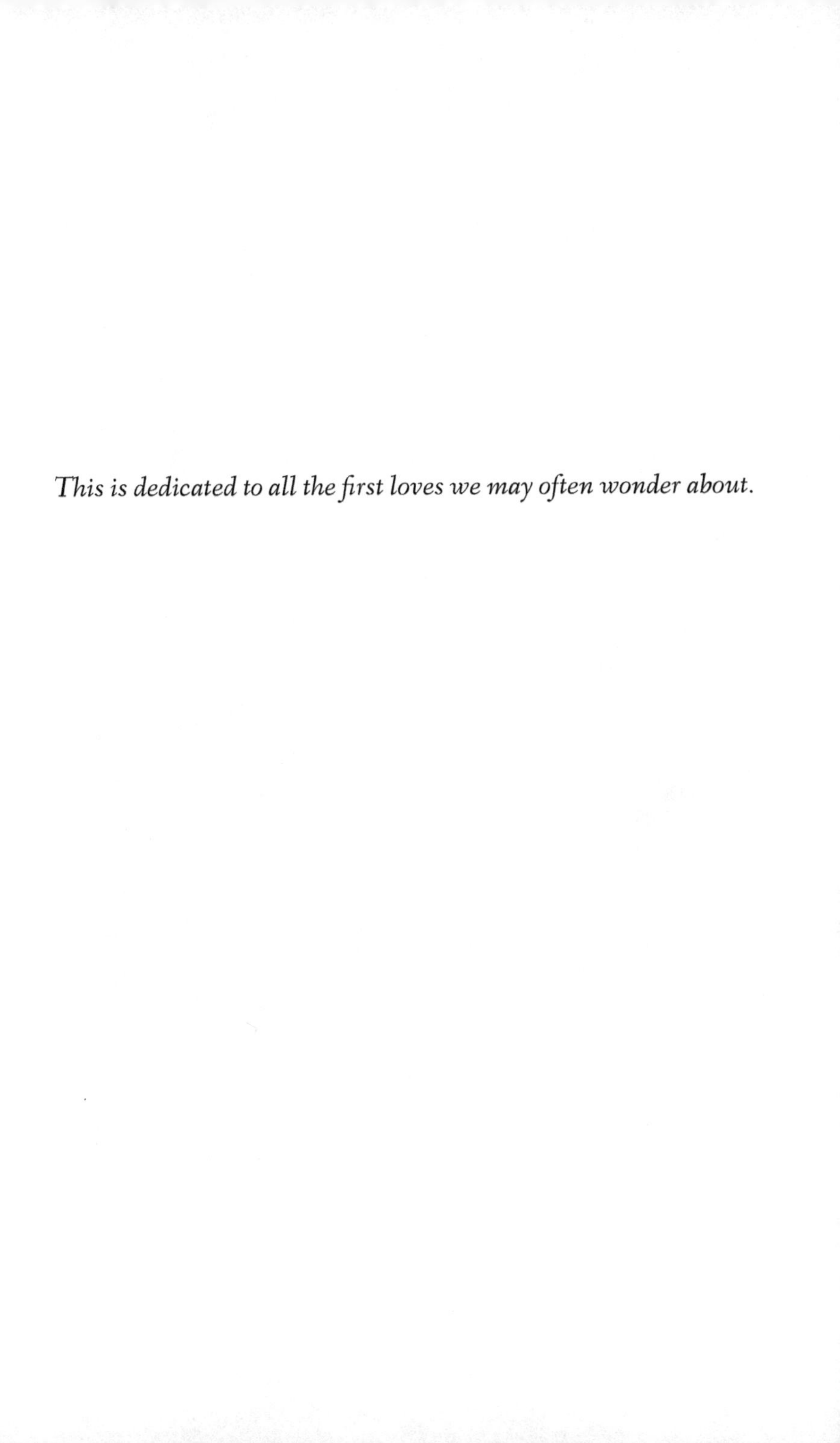

This is dedicated to all the first loves we may often wonder about.

PLAYLIST

Every Other Memory – Ryan Hurd
I Should Probably Go To Bed – Dan + Shay
What Ifs (feat. Lauren Alaina) – Kane Brown
In Case You Didn't Know – Brett Young
Anything But Yours – Rissi Palmer
What Are You Listening To? – Chris Stapleton
Best Shot – Jimmie Allen
Miss Americana & The Heartbreak Prince – Taylor Swift
We Were – Keith Urban, Eric Church
This Is How We Roll – Florida Georgia Line
Heaven – Kane Brown
Love On You – Rissi Palmer
To a T – Stripped – Ryan Hurd
I Go To My Heart – The Avett Brothers
It Would Be You – Ben Rector, Ingrid Michaelson
Die A Happy Man – Thomas Rhett

ONE

JACK

Between the stage lights and the constant dancing (if you could call what I do dancing) and moving around, I was a hot sweaty mess. Sweat dripped down my back and into my eyes. It didn't matter though, because being onstage was electric. It was my sanctuary. The adrenaline and endorphins that ran through my body while I performed made me euphoric.

Bridgestone Arena was packed with fans. It was a sold-out show. The press of people in the pit pushed against the barriers and line of security. Overzealous fans reached out, hoping I'd brush against them, not caring that their perspiring bodies were crushed against each other like occupants of a human sardine can.

Moving my guitar, so it lay on my back, and out of the way, I walked to the edge of the stage and gave them what they wanted. I ran across the front of the stage, running my hand along the row of fingertips that strained outward for the opportunity to have a brief physical connection with me, just so they could brag to their friends later that I'd touched them.

Afterward, amidst their cheers, the song was about to go into the drum and bass solo before the chorus kicked in. I began to clap my hands to the beat Mel was banging out. The crowd mimicked me by clapping their hands in time with mine.

Listening to twenty thousand people clap to the beat of the music was glorious. Then the bass kicked in and a childish grin lit up my face. The music vibrated in my bones. I tapped my foot, enjoying the final moments of the performance.

Now that I had the audience doing exactly what I wanted, I reached for my guitar, and began to belt out the chorus.

After strumming the last notes of the song on my guitar, I looked out and smiled at the crowd. The faces I could see grinned back at me with unadulterated pleasure while they applauded. Hearing them go wild and demand more almost made me give them another encore, but gotta keep them wanting more. I winked and waved my hand high in the air. "Nashville, you've been great. Good night and get home safely."

My band left the stage ahead of me, throwing out kisses and waving to the hyped-up crowd. I was already unhooking my guitar strap before I descended the steps.

Buddy, one of the roadies took my guitar when I exited the stage and threw me a towel.

"Thanks, man." I used it to mop up the sweat that drenched my face and neck.

"Good show tonight." Mel, my drummer patted me on the back.

"Wouldn't be nearly as good without you guys." It was true. My band made me sound incredible, night after night.

"I'll see you guys in PA," I called over my shoulder and kept walking. I was still riding the high from my performance when I entered my dressing room. With the door closed, the crowd could still be heard chanting my name.

"Jack. Jack. Jack."

It was impossible to suppress the smile that broke out across my face. Even though the show had ended, it would take a while for security to empty the venue.

Ten years into my career, and a great concert still made me feel like I was on top of the world. Lately, that feeling didn't last too long once the show was over. Something was missing.

I'd barely been in the room a minute before my assistant, Janine, started talking.

"Danielle called..."

Nothing like hearing an ex you've been avoiding called to put an end to the good night you were having. That chick was batshit crazy. We'd called things off, or rather I'd called things off weeks ago, and she still couldn't take the hint.

"Next." I didn't care to hear what Danielle had to say.

"The pilot is hoping to be in the air no later than noon, so the car will pick you up at eleven o'clock." Janine rattled off tomorrow's schedule. "Your brother called. He apologized. Unfortunately, he can't pick you up from the airport, and won't be able to see you until the day after you arrive."

"That's fine. Can you arrange for a car service? If I know my brother, he's busy saving the world one kid at a time."

Once I took the bottle of water Janine offered, I dropped onto the sofa, and stretched my long legs out, while she droned on.

"You still need to decide on your set for the benefit concert."

After giving her a quick nod to indicate I was listening, I zoned out and thought about the trip home for my ten-year high school reunion. It had been a while since I'd been home. Usually, I flew my family into Nashville or wherever I found myself during a tour. There had never been a need for me to go back.

I'd planned on skipping the reunion until my little brother, Austin, asked me to come home for my reunion and help with a fundraiser for a good cause. He wanted to take advantage of all those people being in town, which was smart. Headlining the event for the organization he ran to help foster kids was a no-brainer. No way I could say no to that. Which is why I was headed home to East Stroudsburg, Pennsylvania, in the Poconos.

"Jack? Earth to Jack. Are you listening to me?"

"Hmm?" I unscrewed the cap on the water and drank down about half. I didn't have to look at Janine to know she was glowering at me for not paying attention.

"Tell me what I just said." The annoyance was palpable and even more pronounced when she pursed her black lipstick-covered lips together and glared at me through her heavy, dark eye makeup.

"You know I wasn't listening, so I'm not gonna lie and tell you I was." I gave her a smirk and didn't bother looking contrite.

She huffed but repeated what she'd previously stated. Some might find her surly demeanor off-putting or rude, but it had been one of the reasons I hired her. She didn't treat me like Jack the Celebrity. She treated me like an average Joe.

Once she finished going over everything, I smiled. "You sure you don't want to come with? The ski resort is pretty nice. I'd get you your own cabin."

"Thanks, but I'm going to stick around here. There's some knitting that I'm behind on."

Many people would have heard that statement and taken one look at Janine and thought she was joking. People often stereotyped her, because of her pale skin, Goth makeup and clothing. She looked somber and intimidating, but she could be a big softie. It had taken no time at all for the guys in the band to warm up to her. Whatever she was knitting was probably for one of them or one of their family members.

"Suit yourself."

Janine went about the room, tidying up things and making

notes about gifts that were delivered so we could send thank you cards. My mind wandered to what this week would hold. Being back in my hometown was going to be like walking into a time warp. Wasn't sure I was ready for who I would encounter. Danielle wasn't the only one of my exes on my mind. Maybe this weekend would be uneventful, and the girl I was thinking of would be too busy to make it to the reunion. Yeah, it was wishful thinking, but a guy could dream right? Was it too much to ask for a drama free week while I was back home?

That was bullshit and I knew it. If there was one girl I would gladly take drama from, it was her. We hadn't seen each other since high school, but as this reunion drew near, she was all I could think about. For four years, she'd been mine until I blew it. After all this time, I could finally take responsibility for what happened. Maybe she'd be amenable to rekindling something between us.

Closing my eyes, I pushed any thoughts of her out of my mind and rested my head against the arm of the sofa. Maybe that was a bad idea. I was too exhausted to think about it clearly. After a show, I was usually ready to crash, which probably was not the best time to decide whether or not to start up with an ex-girlfriend again.

My eyes fluttered closed. I needed to get up and go home. If I got too comfortable on this sofa, I would fall asleep here and there would be no moving me. "Go ahead and have them bring the car around."

"SIR, in ten minutes we'll be landing at the Pocono Mountains Municipal Airport."

Swiping my hand across my face, I looked around the cabin. *I must have fallen asleep.* Were we really already here? Hearing the flight attendant announce our arrival made me feel disoriented. When I got on the plane that morning I'd still been a bit groggy, but the plan had been to decide the set for the benefit concert. On the table in front of me sat an empty notepad. Clearly, I'd accomplished nothing.

I must have fallen asleep shortly after boarding, because I had no memory of the flight. Peering out the window, land and mountains were getting closer as we descended. Once my brain established we were in fact landing, I stretched my arms above my head and yawned. That nap had been just what I needed. I felt refreshed and ready for whatever was waiting for me over this next week.

On the drive to Holiday Springs Resort, I couldn't stop peering out the window. Snow blanketed nearly every surface. Anywhere you looked appeared to be an image worthy of a postcard. This town was beautiful. I'd been away so long I'd forgotten that.

Before I knew it, the SUV was pulling through the large stone pillars that stood at the entrance with a huge metal sign proclaiming the name hanging overhead. *That didn't use to be there.* Back in the day, there had simply been a huge wooden sign bearing the name of the resort. Tires crunched the gravel during the ride through the tall pine trees that lined the road. Memories assailed me of winter nights spent sneaking onto the property to ski after hours or go tubing on the slopes, which wasn't allowed. A small smile of remembrance curled my lip.

Twinkle lights glowed in the trees when we rounded the curb, and the main lodge came into view. I was looking forward to settling into the house I'd rented. After unpacking, I could spend time deciding on the set list for the benefit concert, and maybe even start working on some new songs. The solitude would be welcome, after back-to-back tours and constant traveling.

I exited the car and walked into the lobby. Nothing much had changed. The large, open room was still all stone and wood, with the huge fireplace center stage, for guests to warm themselves around when they came in from the cold.

It only took a second before people turned and stared or did double takes and whispered to their companions.

There was a line at the check-in desk, so I waited like everyone else. I never had any expectation of preferential treatment, nor did I want to be treated differently.

People in the lobby were still whispering, trying to figure out if it was me, by the time it was my turn.

"Hello..." my gaze wandered to her nametag, "Cassie." I flicked my gaze back up to meet hers. The girl looked like she was ready to squeal and start jumping up and down. *Please, God don't.*

Professional decorum must have won, because she only squeaked out a greeting. "Hi."

"My name is..." I began, but then she cut me off.

"I know who you are Mr. Carter..." She blushed and looked down at her keyboard. Quickly, she began to type.

"Just call me Jack." If it was possible, me telling her to refer to me by my first name made her blush even harder.

A few seconds later, her smile faltered a bit. "Umm." Her fingers halted over the keys, while she scanned something on her computer screen.

"This can't be right." This time Cassie gave me a nervous smile.

Something was up. Whatever it was, I was sure I wasn't going to like it. A customer at the counter next to mine had been making a fuss since I walked in and she was still going at it. I hadn't been fazed by it then, but now as I waited for Cassie to tell me what the problem was, irritation settled in my gut at her continuous rant. I felt for the poor woman having to deal with her. The front desk receptionist managed to keep her cool, despite being spoken to like she was a child.

Shifting my stance. I folded my arms and rested them on the counter. "Just give it to me straight, Cassie. What seems to be the problem? I can take it."

She let out a breath. "It seems the Hemlock cottage you reserved, cabin fifty three, was double booked." She gulped and seemed to prepare herself to be bitched at. The customer next to me was doing enough of that for the both of us. Plus, the last thing I wanted was someone in the lobby whipping out a phone and recording me yelling at some helpless woman. Cassie looked like a crier. I'd be an ass to yell at her for something that wasn't her fault. Over time, I'd learned that being kind and reasonable got more accomplished.

"Okay. Things happen. We can get this sorted out. I can move to another cabin. Or maybe they won't mind moving to another cabin. No biggie."

"The thing is, we're all booked up, the hotel and all of the cabins due to the reunion and... and your concert." Her grin returned at the mention of my concert.

"Who do you have me sharing the reservation with? Maybe I can talk to them. Agree to pay for a different cabin or room somewhere else."

Cassie batted her eyes at me for a minute before she looked down at her computer screen. "Umm, her name is Madison Grace."

Before I could respond someone jumped in.

"What? You have us down for the same reservation?"

It had been ten years, but I knew that voice. Even though there was an irritable frustration in her tone, her voice still embodied a sweet melody played by a finely tuned guitar. When I turned around, I couldn't help thinking how adorable

I'd found her in high school. The woman who stood before me now though was smokin' hot.

Glowing brown skin peeked at me from the cleavage of her low-cut top. The tight skinny jeans she wore hugged her ample curves. The natural curls she used to wear were now straightened and lay slightly past her shoulders. When I was finally able to tear my roaming eyes away from her delectable body, my gaze locked with hers. There was a time when those warm, expressive brown eyes used to light up when they looked at me. Now all I saw glaring back at me was hostility.

Despite her demeanor, I gave her a charming smile, hoping to disarm her. "Maddie Grace."

MADDIE

How did life always manage to be so cruel that the first person I ran into upon my arrival was Jack Carter, my former high school boyfriend and the first love of my young heart? Before he broke it.

The bastard.

Of course, with him being the big Grammy-winning superstar he is, I hadn't been able to avoid him as easily as I was sure he'd avoided me. His face was always plastered on some magazine cover, Internet story, on television, or I had to contend with hearing his voice on nearly every radio station. He was never alone either, always with some pretty starlet or up-and-coming country music songbird.

In high school, he'd been the brooding musician who every girl wanted to be with. I was the lucky winner back then, for those four years, until his need for stardom eclipsed what I thought we had.

It was hard not to keep staring at him. He looked like the quintessential country music star, wearing a plaid shirt, jeans that made his ass look incredible and scuffed cowboy boots. All he needed was a Stetson. Those smoldering gray-blue eyes were still the same, but Jack Carter had transformed from lanky boy with a guitar to a sexy, ripped hunk. The five o'clock shadow he sported made him look even more ruggedly handsome than he already was. Looking at his lush, dark brown hair, I was reminded how many times I'd ran my fingers through it during one of his delicious kisses...

You hate this man. Quit drooling over him.

I stalked towards the counter, doing my best to ignore him and push away all the fantasies that were now running rampant in my head.

"What do you mean we're on the same reservation?" Yeah, focusing on the current problem would definitely help get my mind out of the gutter. "I booked this reservation over a month ago."

The girl who was just mooning over Jack now looked flustered under my angry gaze. Her fingers flew over the keyboard, attempting to get answers. I sat my purse on the counter.

Behind me, Jack spoke again. "I didn't know you'd be here?"

Even though I had my back to him, I could feel him towering over me. In my Ugg boots, I topped out at 5'2", so of course his 6'1" frame would eclipse me. If only it weren't still winter, I could be in my four-inch stilettos. At least I'd stand at 5'6" in those.

Why was he standing so damn close?

Briefly, the woman at the counter next to ours distracted me with her ranting. Guess we weren't the only ones with reservation issues. I focused back on the desk clerk. "Well? Have you been able to fix it?"

I was beginning to grow impatient. Between my nerves and anger, I couldn't help drumming my nails against the countertop. I thought I'd have at least until the night of the reunion before I had to lay eyes on Jack. Time to prepare myself, but no. Instead he was now breathing down my neck, and some idiot had managed to mix up our reservations. What were the odds? With the resort being one of the more upscale accommodations in town, I should have known this is where he would choose to stay.

"Sorry... I've tried, but there's nothing I can do. I was just telling Mr. Carter that we're booked solid due to all of the events that are happening this week." The terrified look on her face told me that I was being very intimidating. This wasn't a courtroom or a boardroom so I probably needed to ramp down my anger. If this were a situation that involved any other person, I probably wouldn't be as furious. I certainly didn't mean to be an ass to her.

"It is a two bedroom. Maybe you could share."

When the desk clerk made the suggestion I wanted to tear into her some more. Was she crazy? Jack and I share the cabin?

"No. We won't be sharing anything." Whirling around, I turned to Jack. "Be a gentleman, and let me have the cottage."

That wiped the grin off his face. His eyes narrowed into slits, and he put his hands on his hips. "No."

Of course he was going to be selfish. Why did I think he'd changed? I huffed. "Why not?"

A mirthless chuckle fell from his lips. "You waltz in here and don't even so much as say hello or acknowledge me when I was cordial to you, and now you expect me to just let you have the cabin? It's a no, sweetheart."

He knew just how to get under my skin and irritate the hell out of me. "I'm not your sweetheart." I said the words through gritted teeth.

"Thank God for small favors." He grumbled.

Ugh. I thought Jack looked hot earlier, but now with his nostrils flared and his brows knitted together in an angry expression, I found him dangerously handsome. How could I go from wanting to scratch his eyes out, to wanting to rake my nails down his back in the throes of passion?

Unsure what I was going to say, I turned back to the desk clerk. I was disgusted with myself and needed to take my eyes off of Jack. There was no way I wanted to concede and just let him get his way, but what choice did I have if he wouldn't find another place? I guess it was going to fall on me to be the adult.

Before I spoke next, I glanced at her name tag, hoping that if I was more personable and used her name, she'd go the extra mile to help fix this mess.

"Cassie," I gave her a genuine smile, "I'd really appreciate it, if you could call around and see who has an open reservation?"

"Sure." She nodded and picked up the phone.

My cell phone rang and I stepped away from the desk to answer, knowing exactly who it would be. "I just arrived. I haven't had a chance to check emails... there's a problem with the reservation."

My assistant, Anthony responded. "Madison, I promise everything was correct when I made it over a month ago. I even confirmed it a couple days ago."

"It's nothing you did. Don't worry about it. Somehow the hotel double-booked me. They're full up here, so I'm trying to see if there is a vacancy somewhere else in town." I peered over my shoulder and found Jack watching me.

Rolling my eyes, I turned away from him and walked further away. "Have any of the partners called or emailed to say they needed anything? I have the case files for the Morgenstern civil suit with me."

"No, everyone knows you're out."

"Just make sure they know I'm available if needed. No matter what time it is." I was angling to make partner, so there was no way I would let them think that because I was out of the office I was unreachable. If I were on top of Mount Everest, I would make myself available.

"Yes, of course."

"I'll call you back later, when all of this is settled." I hung up and walked back to the desk. Jack was leaning against the counter.

Since walking into the place it was the first time I noticed that many of the guests were looking in his direction and whispering to each other. He seemed oblivious to it. After ten years, he was probably used to it. As I approached the counter, Cassie hung up the phone. She didn't look hopeful.

"I've called everywhere in town. Nothing's available."

"Damn it." I mumbled under my breath. If my best friend Natalie didn't have a house full of kids, I would ask her to sleep on her sofa, but I had work to do. There was no way I'd accomplish anything there.

"Looks like we're going to be roommates." Jack simpered.

I glowered at him before I turned to Cassie. "Can I get my key please?"

JACK OFFERED to help me with my luggage once I pulled up to the cottage, but I declined. I couldn't stand to see the gloating in his eyes. He was seated in the living room when I finished lugging my bags inside the house.

The living room and kitchen bled into each other, with the wooden kitchen table and chairs acting as a barrier between the two. Plaid curtains decorated the windows on either side of the stone fireplace. Wood paneling covered the walls. A big comfy leather sofa and chairs dominated the space. Off the main area, a short hallway led to the two bedrooms. Jack seemed to sense what I was thinking.

"I didn't choose a room yet. I didn't want you to think I was being unfair, so I waited." He stood. "Ladies first."

Now he was being chivalrous? If he'd wanted to do the right thing he could have found some place else to sleep. His brother, Austin still lived in town. Huffing, I stomped towards the hallway, dragging my bags behind me. When I looked between the two rooms, there weren't too many differences.

"I'll take this one." I walked into the room on the left. The sparsely furnished bedroom contained a queen-sized bed, nightstands, a dresser and a TV. I was thankful each room had its own bathroom. There wouldn't be any long waits or worries about running into a naked Jack.

After I sat my bag on the luggage rack, I closed the door and collapsed on the bed. It was nearing early evening and I was exhausted. I wondered again if I'd made the right decision to come to the reunion. Things were already off to a rocky start. I wasn't sure I could endure a week with Jack.

Okay, Maddie. Now you're being melodramatic. You have dealt with some of New York's toughest litigators and most demanding clients. You can handle your ex-boyfriend for a week.

I took a deep breath and then pulled out my cell phone and texted Anthony to let him know I would call him in the morning. Then I called my best friend, Nat. She answered on the third ring.

"You're here." Her cheery voice instantly made me feel better.

"Yes, and you'll never believe what happened." I still couldn't believe it myself.

"Well, save the story. I just arrived. I knew you would be too busy so I grabbed some groceries to tide you over."

What did I do to deserve such a great friend like her? "You are an angel. You didn't have to do that."

"It's a selfish act. This is my mommy time. I'm free, no kids for a couple hours. Kevin is on duty."

We both giggled. With five children at home I was sure Nat relished every kid-free opportunity she got.

"Which cabin are you in?"

"Fifty-three. I'll see you in a minute." I hung up. Nat was certainly going to have a lot to say over Jack and me sharing a cabin.

Ten minutes later, Nat's van pulled up in front of the cabin. Unfortunately, Jack was already in the living room and was opening the door when I came out of my bedroom.

"Natalie Montgomery? Girl, what are you doing here?" Jack wrapped her up in a big bear hug.

Nat's cheeks were stained a rosy pink from the cold. She wore a headband, holding her blonde locks away from her face. It was clear she was used to the cold, because all she sported was a red sweater, jeans and some snow boots. There was no jacket in sight.

"Jack Carter?" Natalie squealed and hugged him back. "It's Gladwell now... I knew you'd be performing at the concert. I didn't know you were coming in for the reunion as well."

"You married Kevin? How's he doing?" Jack's smile lit up his face while he spoke to Nat.

"He's good, home with the kids right now. He'll be glad to see you at the reunion."

Confusion was written on Nat's face after she pulled out of his embrace. When her gaze locked on mine, she gave me a puzzled look. Questions shined in her eyes, while her gaze darted between Jack and me.

"Honey, do you mind getting the groceries out of the car for me?" She gave Jack an innocent smile and handed him the keys. Nat might have been asking him, but really she was telling him.

I knew she wanted to get rid of him, if only for a few minutes so we could gossip.

"Sure thing." He took her keys and bounded down the steps.

The minute he was out of earshot, she grabbed my hand, and we walked inside the house.

"Who'd have ever thought I'd see Wilmington High's most popular couple together again?"

The teasing tone in her voice made me playfully roll my eyes.

"Explain to me what Jack Carter is doing here. Give me all the dirty details."

We sat on the sofa.

I shrugged. "Reservation mix-up. We were double booked and the resort is full, along with every other place in town, so here we are. Nothing exciting. No dirty details."

"What in the hell? What are the chances that of all the people you could have a reservation mix up with, it would be your old high school boyfriend?"

"I know. The jerk wouldn't let me have the place so I'm stuck."

At that moment, Jack happened to walk back in the door carrying the three grocery bags.

"Well there are a lot worse people you could be rooming with than Jack Carter." Nat mumbled low so only I could hear her, but her eyes followed Jack into the kitchen. Even though I knew she was happily married, I could understand her attraction. Jack was hot. You'd have to be a corpse not to find him sexy.

Nat stood and hiked her purse strap onto her shoulder. "I should be going."

Now I was puzzled. She just got here. What happened to her mommy time? Before I could open my mouth and ask, she edged toward the door and gave me a sly look. "There is a bottle of wine in there. You two should pop it open and have a glass, catch up."

Did she really just try and hook me up with Jack?

"How thoughtful," Jack said behind me, oblivious to Nat's devious, little plan.

Ooh, I was going to get her. I slid my finger across my throat and grinned, before mouthing, *I'm going to make you pay.*

"See the two of you later." The smirk she wore was huge.

After she left, Jack and I silently worked together and put up the groceries. Keeping our mouths shut around one another allowed us to remain civil. It was hard work. I needed a nap.

THREE

JACK

The minute we finished with the groceries, Maddie disappeared into her room and shut the door. The woman was the all-time champion of holding a grudge. Things between us ended less than ideally, but I didn't expect her to still be this angry... okay, that's not true.

If she'd come with me to Nashville, there was a part of me that believed we would have made it, that we'd still be together now.

Cautiously, I approached her door. I raised my hand to knock, but instead stood there with my fist in the air. What was I going to say? Was I going to ask her to unpack the past? Didn't I say I wanted a drama-free week? Why then was I standing outside the door of a woman who clearly hated my guts and wanted nothing to do with me?

You know why. I lowered my hand without knocking.

On a physical level, I still wanted Maddie Grace. My body had responded to her the moment I saw her. Was it possible to look angelic and sinful at the same time? Those bow-shaped lips of hers looked ready for kisses, and the woman had a glorious ass. It looked like it had gotten a little bigger, which I wasn't mad at. I wanted to know what it would feel like filling my hands as I...

Stop it.

Great. Now I was sporting a hard-on from my lusty thoughts about everything I wanted to do to her. A sigh escaped my lips, and I shut my eyes.

With my eyes closed, I saw her looking at me. Maddie always wore her emotions in her eyes: the happy, the sad, the good, the bad, the joy, and the pain. Her eyes always gave her away. Among the hostility and anger I'd seen earlier was the hurt she tried to bury.

When I laid eyes on her in the lobby, I didn't expect my heart to suddenly ache the way it did. I could do something with the dirty thoughts I had about her, but I knew fuck all what to do with these old feelings resurfacing. I didn't stand a snowball's chance in hell with getting Maddie to give me a second chance. Even if I turned on the charm I wasn't sure she'd come around. She wasn't easily fooled.

The bastard in me wanted to knock on her door and start a fight just to see her get angry and argue with me, because the lady was sexy as fuck when she was mad.

What good would come of that? Nothing. Because deep down I knew that I didn't want Maddie to still hate me. I wasn't sure what I wanted, so I turned and walked away. I needed to get out of the cabin before I did something stupid.

It was cold, but I figured the walk to the lodge would do me some good. Cool my blood and the raging hard-on I'd given myself. I pulled the collar up on my coat, stuffed my hands in my pockets, and trudged along the path, trying to think about anything other than the angry woman who was now my room-mate for the next week.

Fifteen minutes later, I found myself in the lobby of the lodge, warming my hands at the fireplace.

"Jack Carter?"

"That's me." I looked at the stocky man with gray at his temples.

A huge grin took over his face and he reached out, took one of my hands between the two of his sweaty ones and shook it. "Christopher Richards. It is such an honor. I'd heard one of country music's biggest acts, and East Stroudsburg hometown legend, was going to be staying with us and I just had to come meet you."

"Thank you." It was the only thing I could think to say at the moment.

Back in high school, when I used to trespass, I remembered a middle-aged couple owned the property. He seemed a little young to have been the owner at that time.

"Didn't an older couple, the Richards used to own this place?"

"Yes, my aunt and uncle. I bought the place from them a few years back." He beamed at me like he'd done something amazing.

For a minute, we stood looking stupidly at each other.

"Oh yeah." He said like he was remembering something he'd forgotten, and nodded towards another man standing nearby. "This is the resort manager, Wyatt Dawson. If you need anything, anything at all, Dawson here will take care of it."

Dawson gave me a subtle wave. The guy looked embarrassed. With my free hand I waved back.

"It sure was a pleasure to meet you." Christopher continued shaking my hand while he spoke. "Looking forward to the concert later this week."

When I looked down at our never-ending handshake, he finally released me. "Sorry about that... well, you have a good night."

As they walked away, Christopher kept looking back over his shoulder at me with a goofy look plastered on his face.

Once they were out of sight, I wiped my hand on my jeans, trying to get rid of the dampness. Then I went in search of the bar.

It must have been too early for most people to be drinking, because the bar was virtually empty. That was just fine with me. It meant less people I had to worry about asking for an autograph. As a celebrity, I was certainly aware that part of the job was taking selfies and signing your John Hancock to bits of paper, napkins, clothing, or the occasional body part, but sometimes you just wanted to be left alone. This was one of those times.

I sat on one of the barstools, and the bartender who'd been flirting with some woman at the other end of the bar approached.

"The name's Zane. I'll be serving you tonight. Did you want to start a tab?" If the guy knew who I was, he didn't let on. I was grateful.

"Gin and tonic. No tab." One drink and then I would head back to the cabin. There was no way I would sit at the bar and have any more than that. People talk and information could be bought. Next thing I knew, I was in the tabloids being painted as an alcoholic.

You learn a few lessons at the beginning of your career. One of those hard lessons was to learn how to hold my liquor in public or drink in private. Now I never had more than one drink when I was out. Often I didn't finish.

While Zane made my drink, a recurring lyric kept playing in my head. I reached for one of the cocktail napkins. "You gotta pen I could borrow?"

Sometimes I kept a small notepad and pen tucked in a pocket, but I'd left them back at the cabin. He placed my drink in front of me, along with my check and a pen. "Here ya go."

I handed him my credit card before I picked up the pen and scribbled down the lyric. Zane ran my card and then returned it to me with the receipt. Using the pen, he'd given me, I signed and left him a healthy tip. My attention was drawn back to the scrawled song lyric that taunted me.

For a few seconds, I stared at the words, before I picked up my drink and took a healthy swallow. I knew it was about Maddie. Shaking my head, I snorted. It hadn't even been twenty-four hours and already she was under my skin and in my blood. It had been that way in high school. Next to my music, my feelings for her had been all consuming. I sat the glass down, my gaze still fixated on the napkin.

Thoughts swirled in my head, while I nursed my drink. Maybe, I should have just let Maddie have the cabin and went to stay with my brother. Wasn't I just torturing the both of us by staying, and not in a good way? *No,* the little voice in my head told me. It was too late. Now that I'd laid eyes on her, and those old feelings had sparked to life, there was no walking it back now.

I stuffed the napkin in my shirt pocket and finished the rest of my drink in one gulp. It was time to go. Before I buried my frustration at the bottom of a glass, or fans showed up looking to buy me a drink.

Roaming around the ski resort grounds, only dredged up more reminders of a different time when Maddie didn't consider me the enemy. At one particular spot, I was reminded of the tomboy who used to challenge me to race her down the hill. A bittersweet smile tugged at my lip. We'd shared some good times. My mind tried to stay away from some of the memories this place evoked. No good could come from reliving those.

The hour grew later, and I was getting colder. It would be

my own fault if I ended up sick. Not to mention, irresponsible, since the concert was at the end of the week. My feet dragged on my way back. I wasn't eager to return to the cabin. With only a wall dividing us, I knew I'd better prepare myself for some restless nights.

FOUR

MADDIE

The alarm on my phone blared. Rapidly, I blinked my eyes and looked around. Once I remembered I was in a bedroom at the cabin, I reached out and turned the alarm off. A good forty-five minute nap always helped me feel refreshed. Now I could get some work done before dinner.

When I walked out into the living room I was greeted with silence. The door to Jack's bedroom was open, which meant he wasn't here. I breathed a sigh of relief. Maybe he would be gone most of the time, and then we wouldn't have to worry about arguing or getting in each other's way.

While the practical part of me saw the benefit of finally having the cabin to myself, there was a small place insidethat I didn't care to acknowledgethat felt a wave of disappointment at his absence. I sat at the kitchen table with my files and laptop and tried to shake it off.

You're being silly.

What's there to miss? He was selfish and made me crazy.

Yeah crazy attracted to him.

No man had a right to look as hot as he did. The stubble is what was driving me wild. It made him look so rugged... along with those hands, his powerful shoulders, the way he looked at me...

I blew out a breath and pushed away my dirty inner thoughts and tried to get down to business. Looking over briefs and depositions should clear my mind of all things Jack Carter.

My head was buried in my computer when the front door opened and closed. I looked over the edge of my laptop screen and watched him cross the living room and walk to his bedroom. It was too early to assume he would stay in there all evening. I went back to my work. Maybe the rest of the night would be uneventful.

Time completely eluded me, as I got lost in my work again. When Jack's bedroom door opened, I assumed he was headed out again.

To my surprise, Jack walked into the kitchen with a towel slung low on his hips and opened up the refrigerator. Leaning on the door, he peered inside. I was trying to keep my gaze on the documents in front of me, but I kept looking up to check out his ass in that towel. Part of me kept hoping it would accidentally fall off. Of course, now I found myself pissed off that, once again, I was having impure thoughts about Jack. I slammed my pen onto the table. "Why are you practically naked?"

Slowly, he closed the refrigerator door and turned to address me.

Damn. Maybe I should have kept quiet. All his sexy goodness was on display for me to see. For a millisecond, I faltered and nearly forgot why I was upset.

"You're not the only one here, you know. We have to share this place..." My tongue darted out and licked my suddenly dry bottom lip. Was his chest and six-pack abs glistening in the light coming from the window, or was I imagining things? *Stop.* "You can't just walk around here half dressed. What if someone showed up?"

"Are you expecting someone?" He wore an amused expression while he asked the question.

I crossed my arms over my chest. "No... but that doesn't matter. Put on a shirt." Why was he so infuriating?

"How would you like it if I pranced around here in my bra..." That had been the wrong thing to say. "Or panties... or nothing at all." I lost steam when I realized the picture I was painting. Being pissed and horny clearly was a bad combination. I wasn't thinking right.

"I don't see a problem." He gave me a lecherous grin that exposed his teeth and revealed his want.

"Have some consideration and stop being selfish." I hurled at him.

That order quickly erased any goodwill he was feeling towards me. His look was thunderous.

"I'm getting real tired of you making me out to be the bad guy here." He gripped the back of one of the kitchen chairs until his knuckles turned white.

"You're asking me to have some consideration?"

The incredulous scowl he wore caused his eyebrows to rise to his hairline. "You're right, Maddie. We are sharing this house. You'd do well to remember that when you crank the heat up to freaking eighty degrees. How about that for consideration? Not all of us want to walk around in a sauna."

He threw his hands up. "It's so damn hot in here, what am I supposed to wear? I'll sweat to death. So unless you're going to compromise on the temperature I'm going to wear whatever I damn well please around here, even if that means I walk around here naked."

I swallowed at the thought of him walking around the cabin naked. Other parts of my anatomy that I didn't care to acknowledge quivered at the thought. Angrily, I stood. "Don't threaten me. It always has to be your way."

Before I knew it, we were yelling over top of each other, trying to be heard. A few minutes later, Jack put his thumb and forefinger in his mouth and whistled, bringing the yelling match to its end. I was so agitated my breathing was erratic. Seconds passed, where we stood glowering at each other like two junkyard dogs that had squared off, but there wasn't a victor.

Jack's shoulders slumped and the fight drained away in front of my eyes. He stared at me, but no longer was his look filled with outrage.

"It's been ten years, Maddie. You gonna stay mad at me forever?" His voice was weary, tired, and bordered on sad.

It wasn't what I expected him to say. I was taken aback by not only his words, but the emotion that lay within his plea. I knew he was trying to get me to meet him halfway, but something in me just wouldn't give in, wouldn't... or maybe couldn't see past my own fury and wounded heart. "I can stay angry for as long as I want. Until I die if I feel like it." Now I was being petty.

Without another word, I stormed out of the room like a bratty kid.

After slamming my bedroom door, I stared at the wood until my vision started to blur. What an idiot I was. I hadn't had dinner, and now I was starving. My stomach gurgled in agreement. There was no way I could go back out there. Not after that little tantrum I'd just thrown.

Ugh.

Way to go, Maddie. Why did I keep letting him bring out the worst in me? I knew that was a cop out. I was a grown-ass woman; how I chose to behave was on me. It was just easier to blame him.

I sank down on my bed and put my head in my hands. Was it going to be like this all week? Bickering and fighting, while also trying to keep my animal urges under control that wanted to just screw him and then go back to hating him? After all these years, why couldn't I let it go?

Something wouldn't let me examine that any further. If I did, I wasn't sure I was ready for the answer. It was one week. I just had to last the week. I grabbed my pajamas from my bag and headed into the bathroom. After my shower, I would go to bed early, and hopefully not dream about angry sex with Jack.

FIVE

JACK

Why was that woman so damn sexy when she was furious? Even though she'd pushed me to the limit last night, I'd wanted to kiss the insolence from her mouth and take her right there in the kitchen. It was a good thing she wasn't awake when I woke up. I wasn't sure I wouldn't try to provoke her.

Despite the argument last night, I'd slept well. After my shower, I dressed in jeans and a t-shirt, and made coffee.

Even though it was winter, I put on my coat, and went and sat on the porch. It was quiet. I inhaled the crisp air and rocked on the porch swing. Drinking the dark brown liquid reminded me of the woman who slept inside: hot and strong.

As a peace offering, I decided to make breakfast for the two of us. When I came into the kitchen, I was once again reminded of how last night ended when I saw her laptop and papers scattered across the table.

It made me smile to myself to see there didn't seem to be any order or structure to what was on the table. Maddie had been messy as a teenager, and it looked like some things hadn't changed.

There was no way I was going to touch her things and have

her take my head off again. Thanks to Nat, I had the makings of a great breakfast: bacon, eggs, and toast.

I was frying the bacon, the item needed to complete the meal, when her door opened.

"That smells good. I'm starving." Maddie stumbled out of her room, rubbing the sleep from her eyes.

The combative woman from last night was nowhere in sight. Or maybe she wasn't conscious enough yet to be hurling insults at me. Either way, I'd take the pleasantness she was serving up.

She wore some silk pajama bottoms and a tank top with no bra. The cabin was toasty, but her nipples stood at attention. I turned back to the stove to finish cooking, so she wouldn't catch me staring.

Seconds later, I pulled some of the hot breakfast meat from the grease and added it to her plate. When I turned around, Maddie plopped down at the table and stretched her arms over her head, treating me to a show of her sexy midriff. I pulled my gaze away and looked from her to all of the clutter on the table, silently indicating that she had to move her things out of the way so I could serve her. It took her drowsy brain a second to understand, but then she piled her papers and laptop together. Once I could see her placemat, I sat the plate down in front of her.

Maddie eyed the plate longingly before she inhaled. "Mmm."

The sound went straight to my dick. I cleared my throat. "Coffee?"

"Yes, please."

I poured her a cup and handed it to her before making my own plate. When I sat across from her, she was still appreciating the food.

A couple seconds passed, and then she picked up her fork

and took a bite. She closed her eyes and savored the bite. "You made this?" She looked at me in disbelief.

"Yeah."

She looked back at her food. I could tell she didn't believe me, which was fair. Back in the day, I could barely boil water. She had a right to be skeptical.

Silently, she ate her food. As time passed, the clearer her eyes became. I could see the thoughts clicking in her brain. I mourned the short time we'd been able to spend in each other's company without fighting. Somehow knowing that it was about to come to an abrupt end.

"Thank you." She offered the gratitude in between bites.

"You're welcome."

Was I wrong? Would today be different? Was she actually going to be civil for a change? Tentatively, I ate my food, waiting for her to yell at me. When she didn't, I decided that maybe now was a good time to ask for peace.

"I was thinking..." I picked up my coffee mug, eyeing her over the rim.

She continued to eat without looking at me.

"What if we called a truce?" Quickly, I drank some of the caffeine, never taking my eyes from her.

For a minute, I wondered if she heard me, because she didn't pause in her eating. She didn't even look up at me. I kept talking. "We're going to share this space for the next week... I just thought it would be nice if we decided that despite the past, we'd be civil to each other. We can even lay down some ground rules. Whaddya say?"

Maddie put her fork down on the edge of her plate. She leaned her elbows on the table and clasped her hands together. Fingers interlocked, she stared at me. It felt like she was sizing me up, while she contemplated my offer for us to make nice with each other. Painful seconds ticked by, where I once again wondered if she heard me.

"Okay."

"Okay?"

She nodded, picked up her fork, and continued to eat her breakfast. I wanted to pump my fist in the air for the small victory I'd just won, but knew that could erase everything. I'd celebrate on the inside.

"Ground rules... what's a rule you want to set in place?" I asked the question before shoveling some eggs into my mouth.

Without needing to think it over, she spoke instantly. "Neither of us can have overnight visitors of the sexual variety."

She didn't miss a beat as she kept eating. I, on the other hand, nearly choked on my eggs. Bringing my coffee cup to my lips and using the hot beverage to clear my airway, helped me recover.

"Okay... good rule." I was being overly agreeable, even though I didn't have plans to fuck anyone else. Maddie was the only woman I hoped to screw before the end of the week.

Did that mean she wasn't seeing anyone? Did that rule mean she thought I was seeing someone, or thought I had plans to sleep my way through the female population of our hometown?

"Is that rule meant for me?" It was hard trying to hide the smirk that tugged at the corner of my lip. Was she jealous?

"I just don't want to have to deal with a bunch of strangers coming and going at crazy hours, that's all." She looked up at me but then averted her gaze. Breaking off a piece of her bacon, she popped it into her mouth and then wiped her hands with her napkin.

"Okay, my turn." I looked up at the ceiling like I was thinking about what I was going to say, but I already knew. "It's clear we're both married to our careers, so my rule is that for this week, neither of us can do any work. We can only have fun."

Her mouth dropped open, and when I was sure she was about to protest, I held up my hand to stop her. "That's my rule, and you have to stick to it. It's just a week. I'm not making a fuss about your rule, you can't make one about mine."

Someone knocked on the front door. We both looked at each other and then at the door. After the second knock, I got up and answered. Austin, my kid brother, stood on the welcome mat, wearing a huge grin. We wrapped each other in a hug. "Hey man. It's so good to see you."

He patted me on the back. "You too."

There was only two years between us. We were both about the same height. My hair was darker. His hair was a lighter brown with blond highlights, but we both had the same gray-blue eyes. I was in really good physical shape, but Austin had played football in high school and college and was still built like a wide receiver. If it hadn't been for a knee injury that sidelined him in college, he probably would have been drafted into the NFL. He never seemed to regret it a day in his life. It was evident he'd found his true calling, which was working with at-risk youth and kids in need.

When he pulled away, he noticed Maddie over my shoulder.

"Is that? That can't me? Mads?" a huge grin broke out across my brother's face.

"Austin." Maddie jumped up out of her seat and ran to him. He picked her up and spun her around. Anyone looking at the two of them would have thought they were the two who dated in high school and not us.

I shut the front door and tried not to choke on the jealousy that suffocated me at seeing how she greeted my brother. "I certainly didn't get that reception." I said the words trying to go for funny, but they came out sounding snarky.

We just agreed on a truce. Don't ruin it.

Pasting on a smile, I took my seat at the table. Austin set Maddie's feet on the ground.

"Mads, how long are you in town?"

While she answered, she sat back down in her chair as well. My brother took the chair next to her.

"Just until after the reunion."

"You're coming to the concert, right?"

Maddie's gaze darted to me before returning to my brother. "I hadn't planned on it."

"Oh, come on, Mads. You have to come." Austin turned on the puppy dog eyes and pressed his palms together, pleading with her. "Please, for me. It's for charity. Come for the kids."

My fork was poised at my mouth, watching the display before me.

"Okay. Okay. You talked me into it." She gave him a shy smile and picked up her coffee mug.

I knew she was mad at me, but I hadn't realized she'd planned to leave right after the reunion.

Before I could stop myself I blurted out what I was thinking. "Do you not listen to my music?"

Maddie gave me a blank look. *Wow.*

"The girl I used to know..." I began, before she abruptly cut me off.

"That's just it. I'm a grown-ass woman. I haven't been a girl in a long time, Jack..." She gave me attitude for days, but I wasn't having it. We'd just made an agreement.

"Uh uh. Truce. Remember?"

Maddie snapped her mouth shut. She swallowed down whatever snarky comment she was about to make and turned back to my brother, ignoring me like I wasn't sitting at the table.

The Maddie I used to know never missed one of my concerts. She used to come to every show, sang the lyrics to every song. I could look out at the crowd of some house party or crummy dive that let me play despite my age and she'd be grinning and singing along. A quick peek at her face, and I saw how animated she was when she talked to my brother. I could feel myself growing grumpier by the second. My breakfast now tasted like ash in my mouth. I pushed my plate away.

When they resumed their conversation, they talked like they were old friends. It was when he asked her about the Morgenstern case that I was pulled from my brooding. I'd just seen that name on one of her papers that she left on the table this morning.

"Do the two of you keep in touch?" I didn't even try to keep the incredulity out of my voice.

They both looked at each other, and then Austin answered. "Yeah, we talk on the phone. When Mads comes into town, we usually have lunch."

The expression they both gave me told me they didn't understand why I was asking the question. To me it seemed pretty obvious: my brother and my ex-girlfriend, friends? No one thought that was strange? I shrugged and sipped my coffee.

Something about the situation he'd walked into must have finally clicked in my brother's brain, because he made the timeout sign with his hands. "Hold up a second. How did the two of you end up sharing a cabin? Is there something one of you wants to tell me?" He looked between the two of us.

"A reservation mix-up." It was evident she was going to say more, but she clammed up and drank her coffee.

I'm sure she was going to tell my brother I was the asshole who didn't want to let her have the cabin. Austin opened his mouth to say something. I kicked him beneath the table, knowing he was going to ask why I didn't just call him and ask to stay. Startled, he looked up at me. He read my look easily, but not before giving me a smug one in return.

Thankfully, Maddie missed the exchange between us. Yeah, I could have called my brother, but then I wouldn't be sitting here with her. I'd been lying to myself yesterday. It wasn't just because I wanted to piss her off, that I forced her to share the cabin with me. I wanted the opportunity to try and make things right between us. Over the years, Maddie had gotten under my skin, like an itch I just couldn't scratch. She was the one that got away.

Now that I'd gotten her to agree to a truce, maybejust maybeI could get her to forgive me.

SIX

MADDIE

It was good to see Austin. When Jack and I dated in high school, Austin and I had grown close. He was like a brother to me. Despite what happened between Jack and me, Austin and I kept in touch over the years.

After I finished my breakfast, I excused myself and went to take a shower, giving Jack and his brother some time alone.

Jack had extended the olive branch, and I would have been a total bitch if I hadn't met him halfway. Truth be told, I didn't want the whole week to be a repeat of last night either. Plus, I'd paid for my tirade going to bed hungry. The breakfast he'd prepared in the morning was so yummy. It really was thoughtful of him.

The only thing I hated about this truce was that he'd said we couldn't do any work? I was not a cheater, but parted of me wanted to sneak my laptop to the lodge and check some emails or get a few things done. If Jack found out I violated the rules, he'd never let me hear the end of it. Maybe I could get him to add on an addendum. Like if one of the partners called and needed something, he had to let me respond.

I finished dressing and stepped out into the living room

expecting to find him there, but the room was empty. He must have stepped out with Austin. I walked to the window and peered out. Austin's car was gone, and I didn't see Jack anywhere.

My fingers were itching to do some work. Jack wasn't here and wouldn't know if I did a little something. *Nope.* It's dishonest. I couldn't do it. No work meant no work. I settled on the sofa and clicked on the TV. After flipping channels, I finally settled on some trashy, mind-numbing reality TV show. Several minutes passed and I was going stir-crazy. Since I didn't know when Jack would be back, and it felt weird sitting around waiting for him, I called up Nat, and we decided to meet for lunch in town at Java Junction.

Breakfast had been pretty filling, so I wasn't terribly hungry. When I arrived at the cafe, Nat was already there. She was bouncing her youngest on her leg when I sat down.

"Hey, cutie." I squeezed, Lizzie's chubby little hand, and she cooed at me.

I leaned over and kissed her on the cheek.

"Hey mama." I said to Nat.

"Hey. I was glad you called. How are things going with Jack?" That topic of conversation seemed to have her full attention

Once I flagged down the waitress, I leaned back in my chair and gave Nat a knowing look. "Last night I thought we were going to kill each other."

This made her laugh. "I have to admit, I was surprised to get such a calm phone call from you today. I was sure you were going to call me from jail and ask me to come bail you out."

That made me laugh. "We came pretty damn close."

"What did he do that made you so angry?" She kept bouncing Lizzie on her knee.

When I looked away, Nat must have noticed something in

my eyes because she scooted to the edge of her seat. "We have known each other way too long, Maddie. I know that look. Spill."

The waitress chose that moment to come to the table. I could have kissed her. It was a brief reprieve, but it bought me some time. There was no way Nat was going to let me off that easily. I perused the menu like I didn't know what I wanted, asking the waitress questions, letting the minutes pile up before I finally made a decision. After both of us ordered a half a turkey sandwich and some tomato soup, the waitress walked away. My time was up. I was going to have to tell her.

Nat gave me a pointed look. Under her scrutiny, I caved. "Okay." A deep sigh fell from my lips. "Last night, I was sitting at the table doing some work, when he walked into the kitchen only wearing a towel."

Nat bit her lip to keep from interrupting me and saying anything.

"I got angry that he was being inconsiderate, and we had a fight."

"Maddie Grace, tell the truth. You were upset with yourself for wanting him. That's why you started a fight."

My cheeks warmed at the truth in her words. Nat was not going to let me off. "Say it."

Lizzie gurgled like she was in agreement with her mother.

"Okay. Okay. I was turned on. There I said it. Jack is totally hot and looks even more amazing after all these years... and, yes, it makes me angry that I'm physically attracted to him."

"Was that so hard?" Nat grinned like a fool.

I glowered at her, but she only snickered.

"Listen, if the itch arises, and it seems like it already has, don't feel guilty..." Nat leaned across the table and in a loud whisper said, "Scratch the itch."

I gave a nervous chuckle and looked away. The last thing I

wanted was my best friend giving me permission to sleep with my ex. Not that I hadn't already had the thought myself.

A short time later, the waitress saved me again. She delivered our food, and then left to wait on some more customers. I didn't want to keep talking to Nat about sex with Jack. I already had a hard enough time thinking about it without her help.

I watched Nat feed Lizzie bits of her food. Suddenly, I was no longer hungry. The rest of the meal, I picked at my food, while we gossiped about some of our old high school crowd that would be at the reunion.

When our meal came to an end, and I got ready to pay, I realized my license was missing. I looked around and under my seat.

"What's wrong?" Nat eyed me with concern while she pulled money from her wallet.

"My license..." I fished around in my purse some more, "it's missing. It's usually right here in the front of my wallet. I drove over here without it."

I could be messy, but I wasn't usually forgetful. Where could I have left it?

"When do you last remember having it?"

In my head, I ran over the scenarios over the last day and a half where I would have removed it from my wallet.

"You know what. I bet I left it at the front desk when I was checking in. I'll swing by the lodge later."

After my lunch with Nat, I didn't want to go back to the cabin just yet, so I aimlessly wandered around downtown. I checked out the flea market, antique shops, even the touristy spots that sold postcards and knick-knacks. Everywhere I walked I was bombarded by flyers promoting the benefit concert. Each one had Jack's grinning face staring back at me. They were stuck to the sides of buildings and on poles, one even got stuck to the bottom of my shoe. The whole point of not going back to the cabin right away was to avoid him. No matter how hard I tried, I just couldn't escape him.

It was getting dark by the time I arrived back at the resort. A trip to the front desk still didn't turn up my license. *Great.*

A light glowed in the living room window of the cabin, letting me know that Jack was there.

When I walked in, he looked up from the TV.

"Hey." He greeted me with an easy smile.

"Hey." I closed the door.

Although he went back to watching whatever was on the TV he kept talking, "How was your day?"

Since he was seated on the sofa, I sat in one of the big leather armchairs. "It was good. I met up with Nat and then just walked around for a while."

Jack used the remote and turned off the TV. I looked over at him wondering why he'd done that.

"I have an idea." His face was full of excitement and glee.

Although, I'd secretly been devising a way I could sneak some work in while on my way here, I was now intrigued by what he was going to suggest.

Something about the way he smiled made me grin. His eyes twinkled with mischief, and it reminded me briefly of the boy I was once in love with. Pushing that thought aside, I leaned forward. Whatever he was cooking up I was in.

WHAT WAS I thinking when I agreed to this? We weren't teenagers anymore. I was an attorney. I was pretty sure the offense for trespassing in Pennsylvania was a hefty fine and maybe some jail time.

Standing on the beginner's slope after hours, holding an

inner tube, I felt a small rush of excitement under the fear and worry that marred my brow. It was just like in high school, except usually Nat, Austin, and Kevin or a few other people would be with us. Occasionally, it had been just the two of us, like now.

"Don't be a chicken," Jack goaded me, pulling me from my thoughts. "Where's that audacious tomboy that used to challenge me every time we came out here?" The grin he wore lit up his whole face. His nose was slightly red from the cold.

"She didn't have to worry about losing her law license." Okay, I was being a bit much. I wouldn't be disbarred if we got caught, but still, I was trying to make partner. It probably wasn't a good look to end up with a mug shot, even for a silly misdemeanor.

Jack started making chicken noises and flapping his arms like a bird. It made me laugh and got me out of my head. "Are you really making chicken noises?"

"Is it working?"

I didn't answer for a moment. Then I gave in. "Maybe."

We both chuckled.

"Let's go together." He suggested.

I looked at him. There was that look in his eyes, that plea, like he was begging to break down the wall I'd erected between us. I looked away and down the slope.

"First one to the bottom is the winner."

Before I could speak, Jack took off at a run.

"You cheater." I cackled and took off after him.

He was down the hill a few seconds before I was, riding the inner tube on his belly. I copied him. It was a rush I hadn't felt for a long time. Even though we weren't supposed to be out there, I found myself yelling into the wind while I whizzed past the trees. I stuck my hands up in the air at my sides, like I was a human airplane, and rode the tube down the rest of the way without hanging on. Of course, Jack reached the bottom first, beating me.

My cheeks burned from the cold, but the minute I climbed off the inner tube I wanted to go again.

"Race you to the top." I shouted and started running up the slope.

"I'm gonna catch you." Jack yelled and gave chase.

I couldn't help it. I started squealing as I ran as fast as I could in the snow, while lugging my inner tube, which wasn't very fast.

I'd just barely made it back to the top when Jack caught me around the waist and tackled me. We went tumbling into the snow. Giggles erupted out of me. Even though I was nearly face-down in the snow, I couldn't stop laughing.

Jack rolled off of me and onto his back. "I forgot how infectious your laugh could be." The huskiness in his voice made my laughter subside.

I looked over at him and was startled to see the longing and lust that clouded his eyes. When he moved closer, I knew what he was about to do. I wasn't sure if I was frozen, paralyzed, or if I simply wanted what he wanted in that moment. I was lying in the snow, but suddenly my body heat felt like it was going to melt the ice beneath me into a puddle. I was about to close my eyes in anticipation of feeling his lips press against mine.

"Hey, what are you two doing out here?" The voice of the security guard broke through the moment we were having. Part of me was thankful. I scrambled to get up. Jack was quicker than me and grabbed me by the elbow and pulled me to my feet.

When I went to grab the inner tube, Jack grabbed my hand. "Leave it."

The security guard's flashlight threw patches of light onto us and the snow at our feet as it bobbed up and down with his movements. Snow and ice crunched beneath his boots while he jogged towards us.

I did as Jack said and left the inner tube.

"Run." The word was wrapped in amusement.

Both of us ran back down the slope towards the path that would take us back to our cabin. It was definitely much easier running down the hill in the snow. Thankfully, we were far enough away from the security guard when he found us that we pulled ahead. We didn't stop running until we were sure he was no longer chasing us.

When we made it onto the porch, we both bent over, gasping for breath. I should have been afraid, and maybe even angry, but I couldn't help laughing again. Jack joined in as well. Walking into the cabin, we were both still chuckling over nearly being caught. I pulled off my jacket and hung it up. "That was fun. I hate we didn't get to slide down one more time."

"Me too." He hung his jacket next to mine.

I walked into the kitchen and headed for one of the cabinets.

"Are you hungry?"

Jack was standing so close when he asked the question. I was trying not to think about what nearly happened between us up on the slope. I actually was hungry, because the last meal I had was at lunch with Nat. Despite that, now that we were back in the cabin, I didn't want to linger out here with him.

Avoiding his gaze, I opened the cabinet and pulled out a granola bar. "Not really," I lied. "I think I'm just going to eat this and turn in early tonight. All that running made me a little tired."

Another lie. I was so wired, but I couldn't stay out here with him and risk something happening, or him wanting to talk about the near kiss. My steps were quick on the way to my bedroom, but then his voice stopped me.

"Hey?"

"Mmmhmm?" I said over my shoulder, not turning around. Nervous energy coursed through me, and my fingers played with the granola bar.

"What about another surprise in the morning? At sunrise?" He sounded hopeful.

I was conflicted. We'd had a lot of fun tonight. I didn't want to spoil things and make things awkward between us by saying no, but I was terrified something would happen between us.

"Are you chicken?"

I wasn't sure if his taunt referred to being afraid to participate in whatever he had planned, or me being afraid to confront what was happening between us?

Without turning around, I gave him answer. "I'm not scared... I'll go."

Yes, you are, you big chicken. That's why you won't look at him.

"Dress warm." His voice sounded deep when he issued the order. It sent a shiver up my spine, and I scampered into my room and shut the door.

I sagged against the door. What had I gotten myself into? I was playing a dangerous game with Jack. He could shatter my heart all over again. Was this just about getting me into bed for old time's sake, or was this about something more? I wasn't sure I was ready to find out.

JACK

After Maddie disappeared into her room, I stared at her door, and let out a breath. Maddie was running away, and I was going to let her run. Part of me was disappointed, and a small part of me felt slightly relieved. Yeah, she'd been puckering those lips and gearing up for my kiss before we were caught, but was I really ready for that? Did I really want Maddie? Or was I just feeling nostalgic because I was back home, and she felt familiar?

Maddie had repeatedly told me she wasn't the same girl I used to know. And I'd definitely matured from the boy I used to be. I knew I better be damn sure I wanted us, before I pulled Maddie into my crazy world.

While I made myself a sandwich, I thought about my feelings and examined them. The more I thought about it, the more I realized, that this wasn't just about me wanting her physically. Trust me, the ache in my balls told me how badly I wanted her but spending time with her on the slope tonight and hearing the tinkle of her laughter, it reminded me how much I cared about her. Hopefully, I was breaking down those walls she'd erected to keep me out. I planned to tear them down until there was nothing that stood between us. At least with no walls between us, we could find out, together, if an 'us' is what we wanted.

After finishing my sandwich, I knew I was still too wired to sleep. TV might help take my mind off of her.

When I dropped onto the armchair I quickly stood because I'd sat on something. It was Maddie's purse. I looked towards her bedroom door. There was a good possibility she was going to leave it out here the rest of the night. I waited a few minutes, listening for any sounds that might indicate she would surprise me and suddenly leave her room.

When I heard her shower cut on, I reached into my pocket and pulled out her license. Earlier, when she left me with Austin after breakfast, I'd lifted it from her purse, needing it for the surprise. Hopefully, she hadn't even realized her license was missing.

I opened her bag to return it but found myself gazing at her photo. Some people took horrible photos for their ID. Not Maddie. In the picture, she wore no makeup, and had her hair in a ponytail. There wasn't a smile on her face, so much as there was a curl to her lip. It was those eyes. Those beautiful, expressive brown eyes, that just pulled you in. The damn woman looked highly desirable. Maybe I was biased. I rubbed my thumb over her picture like a dumbass. It wasn't like I could feel her skin.

I returned it to the slot it occupied in her wallet. Once I put her purse back on the chair where she left it, I went and sat on the sofa. I clicked on the TV and aimlessly flipped through the channels.

A couple hours later, I went to my room. I knew I'd waited up, hoping she might come out of her room, but no such luck. Maybe it was better this way. No, I didn't believe that. That was just the disappointment talking.

After my shower, I lay in bed thinking about her. Reaching

over to the nightstand, I grabbed the napkin I wrote that lyric on and stared at it. There was a song there, I knew it. Tonight, was not the night for me to start writing a song. I had to be up early. I put the napkin back on the nightstand and turned the lamp off. Tomorrow, I needed to put in time breaking down Maddie's walls.

THE NEXT MORNING, it was still dark outside when we emerged from the house.

"Where are you taking me?" She yawned. "We're not trespassing, are we? We can't be arrested this time, right?" The teasing sarcasm in her voice made me grin.

"No, what we're doing this time is completely legit." I turned to her. "The lake's frozen over so I thought we could go ice fishing on Lake Wallenpaupack. February is the best month to go."

"Don't you need a license or permit for that, and gear?"

I stepped to the side so she could see everything sitting on the porch. I'd gotten up a little earlier than her to get it out on the porch for the reveal.

"When did you have time to get all of this stuff?" She eyed the ice fishing rods, bait and tackle, lanterns, folding chairs, blankets, life jackets, sled, and everything else we'd need.

"Where do you think I went yesterday with Austin? He helped me get the licenses and all of this equipment. I already checked the level of the ice. We're good to go."

"Don't we each need a license? I wasn't with you. How could you have gotten a license for me?" Her face was screwed up in confusion.

It was hard not to look a little apologetic. "I borrowed your driver's license when you went to take a shower." I braced for the wrath that was sure to come.

Instead of anger or annoyance, a wave of relief seemed to wash over her. "You mean I didn't lose it?" Maddie started rummaging in her purse and came up with her wallet. She opened it and peered at her license.

"Sorry about that. I was hoping you wouldn't notice it was missing. With your driver's license, I was able to get your fishing license online."

After shutting her wallet, Maddie gifted me with a smile that warmed my insides. "I was so worried I would have to figure out how to get a new one when I'm not in my home state and I don't even have my passport on me... it's a nice surprise." She waved her hand towards the gear.

Well, so far, we were off to a great start.

I looked her over, trying gauge if she would be warm enough on the ice. "Are you wearing layers? It can get pretty cold out there."

"I'm like a snowman right now. I have three layers on."

"Okay."

Maddie handed me the keys to her rental so I could drive. I could have ordered a car service to take us to the lake, but I didn't want anything or anyone getting in the way. If a driver was there, in earshot of what we spoke about, I feared she might be guarded and not be as open. It needed to be just the two of us.

She yawned again.

"Why don't you get inside the car and I'll load the trunk? You can nap on the way, since it's about an hour's drive from here." Maddie didn't disagree with my suggestion. She allowed me to lead her to the car and open the passenger door for her.

It took me about ten minutes to get everything in the car. When I got in the driver's seat, Maddie had her seat laid back and she was sleeping. For a moment, I couldn't take my eyes off of her. I sat there watching her. Back when we were dating, she used to curl up like a kitten and take these quick power naps. I always thought it was cute. Even now, she had her legs tucked into her chest.

Once I was able to tear my gaze away from her, I put on my seat belt and started the car. It was too early for us to encounter nearly anyone out on the road, with the exception of the occasional big rig. In my head, I found the song lyric that came about in the bar a couple days ago, trying to expand and add melodies. Maddie didn't know she was inspiring a song.

I peeked over at her while I drove. The song would probably never see the light of day, so she would never know it was about her. Either way, I couldn't help writing it in my head on the way.

Before we reached the lake, I pulled over at a coffee shop to grab us some coffees to keep us warm and wake us up, while we fished.

The sky was beginning to lighten, and the sun began its slow climb. Purple, pink, and a sliver of orange painted the horizon.

Once we arrived, I shook her slightly to wake her up.

"Huh?" She was still a little dazed when she sat up. "We're here?"

"Yeah."

Right now she was that mixture of sexy and adorable. I wanted to kiss those pouty lips of hers and help her wake up.

When she got out of the car, she stretched.

"Look at the sunrise." I pointed to the sky.

"It's beautiful. I haven't watched one of those in a long time." While she stared up at the sky, I was busy staring at her. I'm sure the sunrise was breathtaking, but she was taking my breath away right now.

Once it was halfway through with its ascent, I motioned to the frozen lake.

"I'm going to go test the ice first. Stay here." I grabbed the drill I'd purchased with Austin and took a few steps out on the ice. So far, so good. I walked out a bit further and then knelt and drilled a couple holes in places, testing the thickness. When I was satisfied that the spot would be okay, I walked back.

"First let's put these on." In the trunk, I retrieved the life jackets and helped her put hers on first, before I put on my own.

Between the two of us, we loaded everything onto the sled and headed out onto the frozen lake. By this point, Maddie was finally wide awake.

On the walk out to the fishing hole, she spoke. "You never took me ice fishing when we were in high school."

"I didn't think you'd like it."

She snorted. "What makes you think I'm going to like it now?"

I shrugged. "I don't know. We're older, more mature. I think you might be able to appreciate it a bit more. Plus, it gives us a chance to talk."

For a while she was quiet. The only noise was the blades of the sled cutting across the ice.

"Are you saying I wasn't mature then?"

We both laughed, and then I answered her. "I don't think either of us were mature then."

It took no time at all to get us all set up. I baited both of our lines when she became squeamish about the worms. When the lines were in the water, she pulled her blanket up to her neck.

Our chairs weren't close together. She was practically sitting across from me on the other side of the hole, and she was doing her best not to make eye contact. A couple minutes passed.

"I'm bored."

"Then let's talk." I stared directly at her.

Maddie stared back at me, but I could see her internally squirming under my gaze. Talking was the last thing she wanted to do. She was expecting me to mention that I was going to kiss her last night, but I didn't.

"Tell me about your love life."

The surprise registered on her face immediately. She wasn't expecting that.

"What's there to tell? I date." She seemed perturbed by the question.

"Yeah, but I bet you haven't been serious about anyone have you?"

Maddie looked away but answered. "What constitutes a serious relationship? Moving in with each other? Walking down the aisle? What?"

She was stalling for time. I would have bet money that none of her relationships had lasted. "How long do your relationships last? A few months? Six? A year?"

Irritated, she pushed to the edge of her seat. "Why am I the one being interrogated? You answer the question." Slowly, she sank back in her seat, the scowl still knitting her brows together.

I took a beat. It hadn't been my intention to anger her. "I was asking, because I think we both like being married to our work, because we're not happy in our personal lives... I date too, but I don't want any of those women."

"So, all those magazines and news stories are just telling lies? Because you look pretty happy to me."

"Pictures can be deceiving. You know that. You're an attorney. Everything isn't what it seems."

"I also know not to believe everything that comes out of someone's mouth."

There was that never-ending anger of hers, directed at me

once again. Was she going to make me keep paying for the wrong I'd done her for the rest of our lives?

"How much longer are you going to stay mad at me about the past?" I leaned forward in my chair. "Better question... why are you still mad at me? What is your version of events that happened ten years ago? Because to me, I felt like we broke up because you didn't want me to pursue music."

A look of shock passed over her face. "Is that how you remember things?" She snorted. "Wow. If I remember correctly, I was at every concert, every performance, at every venue, no matter how crummy or lame. Why would I have not wanted you to go after your dream?"

When she said it like that, I felt like an ass. Maddie had always been supportive, so I remember feeling blindsided when she refused to come with me. What had I missed?

"You want to know what I remember?" She slid forward again and clasped her hands together.

"I remember getting acceptance letters to colleges in New York and California, and you not being nearly as enthusiastic for me as I'd been for you, for so long." She paused.

"I never had a problem with you pursuing your music career. My problem was with the fact that you thought I was supposed to just drop everything and follow you like some starstruck groupie. I had dreams of my own, and it's like you just forgot that. You were angry, because I didn't want to go with you... and I was angry that you were so caught up in your own dreams you didn't see mine."

Shame washed over me. Maddie had been right about me. I'd been a selfish dick. It had been a while since I thought about the last night, we saw each other. I remembered there were tears in her eyes, and being the arrogant prick that I was, I believed they were for me, and the demise of our relationship. Now I realize they were tears of disappointment that, after all that time, I hadn't seen her.

"I was a stupid kid then... I know that doesn't erase how I made you feel then, but... I'm sorry that I made you feel small or like what you wanted didn't matter to me. I was so caught up in there not being an us anymore, and blinded by my own grief, that I couldn't see you were hurting too. I'm not trying to make excuses, but that's the truth. I'm really sorry I hurt you."

Part of me couldn't believe I was pouring my heart out to her right now, but if not now, when? This needed to be said.

"Every day of that first year we were apart, I would pick up the phone like ten times a day to call you, but I could never go through with it. I was so miserable, I actually lost the first small contract I got..." I chuckled remembering that period.

Her jaw dropped open upon hearing that.

"The guy told me my music was too sad... I missed you... I guess that's the trouble with falling in love so young, but also having big dreams."

Maddie remained quiet throughout my soul sharing. I wasn't even sure if she accepted my apology. Well it was either go big or go home, so I decided to drop one more truth bomb on her.

"I've been walking around with this hole in my heart for a long time. Seeing you that day in the lobby, despite you hating my guts, it made me feel like I might get a do over... that my heart might be made whole. It felt like you might have been experiencing the same thing. Maybe I'm wrong. I don't know. Either way, at least I was able to try and make things right between us, because I want you to be happy..."

Neither of us said a word. I still wasn't sure if she accepted my apology or not. Fifteen minutes passed before I looked at her again. Her lashes were spiked with tears.

Suddenly, I felt contrite. "I didn't mean to make you cry, Maddie girl." I said the words softly.

I hadn't used my nickname for her since we were together, but somehow it felt right. If she told me not to call her that, then I wouldn't. I waited.

"You didn't make me cry... I'm crying because I'm so cold."

"Why didn't you say something sooner? Come here." I commanded her.

"No. I'm okay." She sniffled and tried to burrow further into her blanket.

"No, you're not. I said come here."

Grudgingly, she got up from her chair, still swaddled in her blanket. I could hear her grumbling under her breath.

"What was that?" I raised an eyebrow at her, while staring at her face.

"Nothing." She pouted.

I lifted my blanket from my lap and motioned for her to sit down.

"I'm not going to sit on your lap, Jack." She tried to retreat back to her seat, but I caught her wrist and held her.

"You're cold. My body heat and the extra blanket will keep you warm." I pulled her down onto my lap, and draped my blanket over the two of us. I spread my legs wider apart, so my thighs would cradle her. I hoped the layers she was wearing would keep her from feeling the hard-on I now sported from having her in my lap.

At first she sat so stiffly, I wasn't sure she would ever relax. With each passing minute, her body gradually molded itself to mine until she reclined against me. A tremor ran through her body. I wasn't sure if it was in response to the cold or to me.

Rubbing my gloved hands up and down her arms, I hoped to quell her shivering. "Better?"

"Yes." Maddie shifted around a bit more until it seemed like she was comfortable. After a few more minutes, I wrapped my arms around her and tucked her head under my chin. She didn't protest or try and put up a fight. I wasn't certain, but I thought I heard her sigh.

We both sat silently stewing in our own thoughts for a long time.

"I accept your apology." She said the words so softly I almost didn't hear her.

I held her a little tighter.

"I lied earlier." Her voice was small. "It wasn't just the cold that made me cry."

There was no need for me to ask her to elaborate or explain. It was enough for now. I was happy she allowed me to hold her.

Today, with my apology, I hoped we could start a new chapter, and turn the page on the past. Maybe now, Maddie would finally be agreeable to something other than just friends.

EIGHT

MADDIE

The night before, I'd spent so much time worrying about the near kiss, I'd been totally unprepared to deal with the truth Jack spilled all over the ice while we fished. I secretly felt like he got me out there, in the middle of nowhere, so I couldn't run away.

I had no words for him. It felt like I owed him as much as he gave me, but I wasn't ready. As I sat in his lap with his warmth surrounding me, I wasn't cold anymore, but it didn't mean he'd completely thawed my heart towards him.

It was a little scary how close he'd come.

We only stayed out on the ice for a few more hours. By the time we decided we'd had enough of fishing, we'd caught a trout and a couple of perch. On the way back, I pretended to fall asleep to avoid having a conversation.

I know. I was a coward. It's just I didn't know how I felt. Part of me was still reeling from Jack's confession. He wasn't wrong though, about me. None of my relationships had been serious. I was married to my work. It was why I was willing to work the whole time I was on vacation, so I didn't have to be reminded how empty my life had become.

I enjoyed my job, but coming home to an empty house was

sad. Most of my colleagues and the few girlfriends I had were starting to get married and have babies.

"Maddie, we're back." Jack shook me awake.

The drive back felt shorter. I guess that's what happens when the whole car ride is spent musing over things in your head. I pretended to stretch and yawn.

As we unpacked the car, I asked about the fish. "Who's going to clean the fish?"

"We are." He responded.

My eyebrows went up into my hairline. "We are?"

Jack laughed at me. "It's not hard, and I promise it won't be as disgusting as you're thinking. I'll show you."

I had to say I was still shocked over this new domesticated Jack that enjoyed cooking. He'd maybe been decent at putting together a peanut butter and jelly sandwich when we were younger, but anything that required a flame ended up burned.

Once the gear was left on the porch, I went to clean up before I joined Jack in the kitchen. He was already wrist deep in fish guts when I returned.

"Come here. I'll show you how to gut a fish and then debone it."

That was the second time he'd commanded me to do something, and I have to say, I found it kinda sexy.

He handed me a knife, and made space for me at the counter. With the patience of a saint, he began walking me through the steps. At first, I watched while he demonstrated, enjoying how skilled his hands were at handling the delicate meat, ensuring it didn't rip to shreds during the process.

I was reminded of breakfast the other day and how tasty it was. And now Jack could gut and debone a fish like he'd trained at Le Cordon Bleu? It was hard not to be turned on by him. The man could sing, cook...

Don't go there.

I focused back on the fish.

"Ready to try?"

Damn it. I'd been so busy fantasizing about him. I'd missed the last step. I simply smiled and nodded and took the fish in my hands. Everything I was doing was wrong.

"Here let me show you." Jack stepped behind me, pressing his chest into my back, and he reached around and set his hands on top of mine. The gesture was so intimate. If he felt anything I didn't notice, because he started maneuvering my hands into the correct positions to ensure I would do everything properly.

Flames licked at my insides, and my body temperature spiked a couple of degrees at his nearness. His deep voice rumbled in my ear while he talked through the movements, moving the blade through the skin.

"Grip the tail firmly... yeah, just like that. Now slide the blade inside..." Was Jack aware how the words sounded? Who knew filleting a fish could be so erotic? The blurred lines of gutting a fish and sex had me horny.

Jack must have felt the same way too, because I felt his dick harden. He cleared his throat and stepped away from me.

I was all hot and bothered now. "I think Nat said there was a bottle of wine. Why don't I open that?" I needed air. I was about to melt into a puddle on the floor, and it wasn't because the heat was on in the cabin.

Jack handled the rest of the meal preparations, while I supervised and guzzled wine. We kept it to witty banter and light conversation. It was nice. The conversation continued to flow through lunch. We caught up on each other's lives, and there wasn't an expectation of anything more.

After the meal, while we were cleaning up, I was trying to figure out something that would keep us in each other's company.

"It looks like Nat included items for s'mores in the groceries she gave us. I'll start a fire, and we can toast the marshmallows?" Jack looked at me expectantly. I guess I wasn't the only one searching for a reason to keep things going as they had been.

A smile tugged at the corner of my mouth. "I'll grab hangers from the closet."

I retrieved the hangers and sat cross-legged on the floor, next to Jack, in front of the fireplace. A nice blaze was going. The smorgasbord of marshmallows, chocolate, and graham crackers sat on the coffee table, along with another bottle of wine.

Jack popped a marshmallow into his mouth. I handed him over the hangers, so he could straighten the wire. While he did that, I plucked a marshmallow from the bag and ate the treat. When he finished bending the wire into skewers, he put marshmallows on the end of both and handed me one.

I was beginning to grow comfortable with the silences we often found ourselves in. Side-by-side we watched the fire leap up and lick the white confection until it turned a golden brown. I kept rotating my skewer so that the flames toasted the marshmallow evenly. I sipped at my glass of red.

Jack pulled his from the heat and blew on it, before reaching for the other ingredients.

Seconds later, I pulled mine out and blew on it. The glob that hung from the end of my hanger looked like it was going to fall off. I wasn't sure what I was thinking, but I reached up to steady it and my thumb touched the heated metal.

"Aww." I dropped the metal coat hanger on the ground and grabbed my thumb.

"What's wrong?" Concern was etched into every plain of his face.

I winced. "I think I burned my thumb." I cradled it with my other hand, willing the stinging pain away. It must have been the wine. I wasn't usually this clumsy.

Jack set his coat hanger with his marshmallow on the table and scooted closer. "Let me see."

"It's okay." I tried to resist when he reached for my hand.

"Maddie, let me take a look." His gaze locked on mine. I was being foolish. He was trying to help, and I was being stubborn. I nodded and let him take my hand. His head hung over my lap while he peered at my thumb.

"Come on. We need to run cool water over it for about twenty minutes."

We stood together and walked into the kitchen. Jack turned on the faucet and adjusted the temperature before he set a timer on his watch. He was being so attentive. I couldn't take my eyes off of him, while he was so focused on my burned skin.

"Ow." I tried to pull my thumb away when the water hit it.

Gently, he took my wrist and kept me from pulling my hand away. Our eyes connected again. "I know it stings a little but you're going to have to hold it under here for twenty minutes."

I looked away again and grimaced in pain before biting my lip. "I'm being a big baby."

"No, you're not. You want to know why I knew what to do?"

I nodded. I knew he was trying to take my mind off the pain, and the fact we would have to stand here for nearly half an hour. "Earlier you asked me how I learned how to cook so well." He paused lost in some long ago thought. "When the first album hit big I bought a house, and it had this expensive chef's kitchen that I couldn't use..." He stopped, seeming to get lost again in some memory.

"Sometimes, during interviews I tell them I learned to cook, because I wanted to impress a girl..."

He chuckled and then smiled a sad smile. "Maybe there was some truth to that." The look he gave me after saying that let me know he was talking about me. I swallowed. Why did he have to keep looking at me like that?

"Anyways… I needed a hobby, something to do, and I had this really nice kitchen, so in between writing music and performing, I learned how to cook. I suffered many burns at the beginning, but once I started to master certain techniques, cooking became very therapeutic."

After he told that story, we both fell silent. Only the sounds of the running water and the crackling fire filled the room. About a minute later, Jack began to hum. I knew the song.

"Is that, 'Every Heart Breaks?'"

Jack sported a toothy grin, and his eyes were lit up in amusement. "So you do listen to my music?"

"I never said I didn't." I tucked a strand of hair behind my ear. "You assumed my silence the other day meant I didn't listen to your music."

"Is that your favorite song?" He peered at me.

I giggled. "Stop fishing for a compliment. I listen to your music. You should be happy with that."

Since we were talking about his music, I decided to ask him another question. "Are you going to sing that song at the benefit concert?"

The broad grin exposed his teeth, and he chuckled again.

"I know you're enjoying this. Just answer the question." I shook my head.

"Do you think I should sing it at the concert?"

I was surprised by his question. Why did my opinion matter?

"What other songs do you think I should sing?"

Now I knew he was just trying to test my knowledge. See how much of his music I actually knew. He pursed his lips, trying to suppress his laughter while he watched me and waited for an answer.

Since I'd already admitted I listened to his music, I decided to wow him. "Well since you're asking… I would start the show off with the party anthem one that everyone was rocking from your second album..."

"'Let's Party Every Night?'"

"Yeah, that one. Get the crowd hyped. Then I would follow that with "'Every Girl's a Tease'..."

"Really?" He wrinkled his nose.

"Trust me. Every woman I know loves that song. After that, switch gears and do 'Hey Lover,' 'My Mama Raised Me Right,' and your last song should be 'Every Heart Breaks,' since it's such a powerful ballad. Actually, make that you're next-to-last song. I would sing 'Give Me Your Love,' for the final song. It's considered a ballad, but it's a little more hopeful and upbeat."

For a minute, he stood there gawking at me with this goofy look on his face. "I have to say. I'm really impressed with your depth of knowledge in regards to my song book." Jack smirked before looking at his watch. Something must have occurred to him, because a weird look crossed his face and then he looked at me directly.

"Have you ever been to one of my concerts?" His eyes got big when he asked the question.

I looked away. I wasn't going to answer that one. The timer on his watch started to go off, alerting us that the twenty minutes was up. I yanked my hand from under the faucet.

Jack clicked the button on his watch, and then turned off the water. Before I could stop him, he took my hand and cradled it between both of his while he peered at it, continuing to play doctor. "I think I packed some aloe vera gel. Some kind of lotion should be rubbed on, to further soothe it."

Before I realized what he was doing, he brought my thumb up to his mouth and kissed it, lingering for a few seconds. I was speechless, and even though he'd only kissed my thumb, I was a little turned on. Once again, I was going to blame the wine for my reaction.

When he looked at me, I held his gaze. I was terrified we were about to have another moment like last night on the slope with the near kiss, so I blurted out the first thing that popped into my head. "I know we set the rule about no work, but I really should check in with my assistant."

The look on his face told me he was about to find an excuse for why I shouldn't worry about work, so I rushed to keep talking. Hopefully, it would persuade him.

"With many of the reunion festivities taking place tomorrow, it would really help not to have any work hanging over my head."

Jack released my hand and gave me an easy smile. "That's not a bad idea. I should probably check in with Janine about some things. Plus, I have this song lyric that's begging me to work on it."

"Okay then."

On the way towards my room, I looked back over my shoulder at him. He'd walked into the living room to clean up our failed s'mores. I wasn't sure why I was resisting him so hard. Once again, I'd run like a coward, and I had no plans to resurface the rest of the night.

When I went into my room and shut the door, I pulled out my laptop and the files from the Morgenstern case and started to work. I did have a pile of emails, but thankfully, nothing was urgent or pressing. A couple hours later, I fell asleep. When I awoke it was dark outside. I wasn't sure how long I slept.

I poked my head outside the door and found it dark in the living room. Jack's door was closed. I tiptoed into the kitchen and grabbed a snack to take to my room. On the way back, I realized Jack wasn't asleep. The sound of him playing his guitar came through the closed door. I knew I was eavesdropping, but I stood outside his door for a minute and listened. Each note he plucked and chord he strummed sounded sad. I pressed my hand to his door for a brief moment.

Several minutes later, I turned to head into my room, and realized there was something laying to the left of the doorway. I stooped to pick it up. It was a tube of aloe vera gel. When I stood, I briefly glanced at his door again. Turning the gel over in my hands, I couldn't help but think about Jack. I wasn't giving him enough credit. He'd changed too. Here he was trying to reach me, and I kept him at arms-length.

Tomorrow was the reunion. Part of me was glad this week was almost over, and the other part of me wanted more time. I was straddling the fence, and I needed to make a decision.

NINE

JACK

I never remembered Maddie being a runner. Every time shit started getting real between us, she took off. How could I show her I wouldn't break her heart again? I wasn't that same kid I was when we were teenagers.

Maddie had left the room at some point during the night, because the aloe vera wasn't there when I walked out of my room. Guess that counted for something, right?

She spent the majority of her morning locked away in her room. Maybe she was working. I didn't know. I'd been hoping to talk with her before we had to leave for the reunion, but it didn't look like she was going to let that happen. Yeah, I could have knocked on her door, but something was holding me back from chasing her. I was sure it was my pride.

Instead of spending the day waiting to have a conversation I knew Maddie was avoiding, I left the cabin and went to have lunch in town. I wore a baseball cap to avoid being recognized right away. When I returned to the resort, I went for a walk and tried not to think about her, but it was impossible. After nearly an hour, I checked my watch and realized I should head back and get ready for tonight.

I CHECKED MY WATCH AGAIN. It was now five o'clock. We were officially going to be late. Maddie had all day to get ready but was still primping and putting on make-up or whatever women did to get ready.

I let out a deep sigh and checked my watch again, knowing it had only been three minutes since the last time I looked.

Her bedroom door opened. I stood and turned to watch her enter the living room. She took my breath away. Since it was winter and we'd spent so much time outdoors, I'd only seen her in sweaters and bulky clothing, which she still looked sexy in. The woman could wear anything. But when she stepped out of her bedroom, I was blown away by how stunning she was. Her hair was up in this messy, sexy updo. The short, black lace dress she wore hugged her curves. She had on black tights and some stiletto ankle boots.

"Sorry." Maddie offered the apology while she put in her earring.

"You look... you look great."

She stood a little straighter, and her face lit up with a dazzling smile. "I do?"

Usually when a woman says that, I know she's just somehow expecting me to compliment her again, but I knew Maddie didn't understand how beautiful she was.

"Yes."

"Oh wait, I almost forgot my purse." When she turned to walk back into her room, that's when I saw the dress was backless.

Dear God, I didn't think I was going to be able to keep my hands off that woman tonight. She returned to the living room with her clutch. I held her jacket for her, while she put it on.

"I'm sure we're going to have a lot of people talking tonight."

"Oh yeah?" I played dumb. "Why is that?"

Playfully, she rolled her eyes. "You know why... we used to date, and as far as most people know, we broke up, and you've been dating models, singers, and actresses. Then we show up at the reunion together? What's everyone going to think?"

"What do you think everyone's going to think?"

Maddie gave me a coy look. "We should go. We're already late."

And whose fault is that?

I wanted to say the words aloud, but there was no way I was going to antagonize her.

In the car, we turned the radio on and let that fill the silence. I drove her rental towards our old high school, wondering what was going on in that head of hers.

When we pulled up in the parking lot, I was assaulted by a ton of memories, many of which included Maddie. Unfortunately, I didn't get the chance to take a trip down memory lane with her before we headed inside, because she opened the door and got out. It was on the tip of my tongue, to ask her if she remembered making out in the backseat of my father's car in this lot, or recalled Senior Ditch Day when me, her, Nat and Kevin nearly got caught by the principal trying to bust Austin out of class so he could spend the day with us.

She peered inside the open car door. "You coming?"

"Yeah." I opened the driver's side door and exited the car. Ten years later, and the school still looked the same.

There were a few other people walking in late like us. We walked side-by-side across the asphalt, and I had the strong urge to take her hand like I used to all those years ago. I looked over at Maddie. Of course, she was looking straight ahead. I focused my attention back on the entrance, which was decorated with streamers and balloons.

In the lobby, Nat was seated at a table with a couple of other people who had been on the student council our senior year, handing out name badges and signing people in. The minute she saw the two of us, she jumped up from the table and rushed towards us.

"Look at the two of you. I know who all the gossip is going to be about tonight." She teased us, and somehow I knew she was going to be the one to start most of it.

Maddie gave me an "I told you so" look. I just shrugged my shoulders in amusement. Let them talk. There were much worse things than gossip. If they wanted to believe Maddie and I were a couple or had gotten back together, I personally didn't see a problem with that.

Nat linked arms with Maddie, and walked to the check-in table. I trailed them smiling and nodding at former classmates who passed by.

After Nat signed us in and handed us our name badges, we headed into the gym. Music from our time in high school blared loudly. The room still had a stale smell of sweat, body odor, and chewed gum, which they'd tried to cover with some sort of industrial air freshener. I wrinkled my nose.

"Do you want a drink?" I asked Maddie.

She looked at me strangely.

"What?"

"This isn't... a date. You don't have to wait on me..." She looked around like someone might overhear our conversation.

Now I was fucking irritated. I'd been putting up with her lack of giving me a straight answer, or even a hint of how she felt. And now I had to deal with this high school bullshit. Was Maddie really concerned with these people from high school, who we hadn't seen in ten years, weighing in on whether we did or didn't have a relationship?

"I'm not some crappy date you got stuck with, Maddie, and we haven't been in high school in a long time. We drove here together. I'd like to think that, even though you can't tell me how you feel about me, that we're still friends. And when friends attend an event together, they get each other a drink throughout the evening, without it meaning something." My blood was boiling and I knew my voice had gotten a bit louder in my anger. Honestly, I didn't care. "Since you're so concerned with what everyone else here will think, why don't I just eliminate the problem for you."

I stomped off to the punchbowl without waiting to hear her response. Standing next to the refreshment table was Tyson Mitchell.

"Hey man. How's it going?" We shook hands.

I remembered he was an Olympian. We chatted for a while about what had been going on. Part way into our conversation, the DJ decided to play my song, "Let's Party Every Night." Inwardly, I cringed. It was like the song was a sign for all the guys who had been complete tools to me in high school, because I didn't play football, to come over and start telling me they were big fans.

Tyson gave me a knowing look. I knew he understood what it was to be in the limelight and have everyone pretend to be your best friend. It would have been easier to endure this with Maddie by my side. Maybe I overreacted. It's not like I hadn't known she was skittish about us. I acted like a jerk.

I looked around the gym but couldn't spot her.

Someone jumped on my back and started laughing hysterically before landing back on the ground. "Nat said you'd be here, but I didn't believe her."

Kevin stepped in front of me. I was relieved to see him. We were actually friends in high school. He'd gained a little weight and lost a little hair, but he sported that huge grin I always remembered. Some of the assholes wandered away.

"How's it going?" He clapped his hand on my shoulder.

"I didn't think I'd be here again." I looked around the gymnasium reliving some moments from high school. This time the memories were not fond ones.

We both laughed.

"Nat told me that you and Maddie ended up sharing a cabin together? How's that going? She still hate your guts?" Leave it to Kevin not to beat around the bush. It was definitely evident why he and Nat had always made such a great couple. Neither of them had a filter or tiptoed around an issue.

Even if I wanted to answer his question though, I couldn't have, because I didn't know.

TEN

MADDIE

When Jack stalked away in anger, I wanted to go after him, but I didn't. I didn't care what these people thought. Most of them I hadn't seen since high school, and most I hadn't even been friends with when I was here.

"Madison Grace?"

I looked up to find a girl who looked vaguely familiar, but I couldn't remember her name.

"Elise Jensen." She placed her hand over her chest. "I wasn't sure if you remembered me. We were in Mr. Townsend's physics class together senior year?"

Truth be told, I didn't remember her.

"Hey." I put on a fake smile and shook her hand when she offered it. I wasn't sure why I didn't just tell her I didn't remember her. Maybe I wanted to spare her feelings.

"What have you been up to since graduation?"

"Went to Columbia for both undergrad and law school. I'm an attorney now. What about you?"

"Daniel and I got married shortly after high school, and when the first baby came along, I dropped out of college to be a stay-at-home mom. Daniel took over at his dad's dealership a while back. We have three kids now."

"Wow. That's... great."

Who was Daniel? And why hadn't I just told the truth about not remembering her? Then I wouldn't be trapped in this conversation.

I awkwardly grinned at her. *Somebody save me.*

Elise was about to say something else when a vivacious blonde wandered up who I instantly recognized. Noreen Hamilton. She'd been the resident mean girl. As expected, she had her pack fall in line behind her, each one her carbon copy. Elise gave me a nervous smile and then slipped away before they could approach.

"Madison Grace?" Noreen eyed me up and down with disbelief shining in her eyes.

Let's just say in high school, I hadn't been known for my fashion sense.

"Wow. Some people really improve after high school."

Her minions snickered. She gave me a snarky smirk, like we were in some teen movie and I was going to get all weepy over her comment. Clearly, she hadn't gotten the memo that we were all adults. Maybe this scenario was what she still needed to feel important. Who knew? I didn't really care. I just wanted her to say what she came over to say and keep it moving.

"What do you want?" Unlike Elise, who seemed like a sweetheart, I wasn't going to entertain Noreen's need to reign supreme. We never ran in the same circles in high school. I stayed out of her way, and she stayed out of mine.

Before she could chime in, one of her bobble-headed minions spoke up first. "We saw you and Jack arrive together. Isn't he dating a model or an actress?"

Noreen shot her a death glare, and the woman stepped back

in line, looking apologetic. When Noreen turned back to me, she was sporting the fake saccharine smile again.

"So, are the two of you together?"

I should have known that's what this conversation was about. Now that Jack was a huge, successful singer, Noreen was hoping she had a shot. In high school, I knew she found him attractive, but at the time he didn't fit her mold of the cookie cutter image she had for her future.

Despite one of the other women already being reprimanded by Noreen for speaking up, the bubbly one chimed in. "Everyone thought that you and Jack were going to go all the way. Get married and have a bunch of cute babies."

Once upon a time I'd thought the same thing as well.

I looked across the gymnasium where Jack was encircled by some of the same clowns who used to give him a hard time. He looked uncomfortable, and slightly miserable. Just like me. We'd been the misfits in high school. That was one of the things that had always drawn us together. If only I hadn't opened my big mouth earlier, we'd be suffering through this together.

"Stop interrupting me." Noreen snapped. She took a deep breath and then addressed me again. "Are you guys an item again?"

I shook my head. "No. He just gave me a ride."

"Do you know if he's single? Is he here alone?" Before I could answer any of her questions, Noreen was already looking in his direction.

"If so he won't be leaving alone." One of her pack made the comment and they all started to giggle.

I rolled my eyes and walked away. Nat was able to grab a half an hour with me, but since she was on the reunion committee, she had duties to attend to.

Why had I even come to this? I could come visit Nat anytime. She was the only person, besides Austin who I even kept in touch with from town. Plus, my parents had moved away years ago.

I looked over in Jack's direction again, and this time he was with Kevin, smiling and laughing. *Oh yeah.* That's why I came to the reunion. Even though I'd still been so angry with him, I'd wanted to see him.

The evening wore on, and Jack had not spoken to me since he stormed away. I felt like an idiot. Here I was worried that someone would think that we're together. What exactly was wrong with that? I stood near the hor d'oeuvres table, really thinking about what Jack had said. It was my own fear that was causing me to act irrationally. I didn't want someone putting a label on our relationship before I had a chance to define what we were for myself. The last thing I wanted was to be pressured by Jack or anyone else to decide what we were.

Yes, it was taking me longer to reach a decision on what I wanted that to be. I was being calculating and guarded, and weighing all the pros and cons. It's these traits that had kept me from being hurt again, and one of the reasons I loved practicing law: logic, reason, black and white. There was usually always a clear answer and very few gray areas. I didn't have to rely on my heart to make a decision.

Jack led with his heart. He'd always done that. It just wasn't my way. Not anymore, not since he broke me. I wrapped my arms around myself.

Nat's voice rang out across the gym. "Okay everyone..."

When I looked up, she was now on stage. The DJ stopped the music.

"It's now time to announce the Reunion Prom King and Queen." Nat's voice was full of excitement.

Some people applauded and cheered.

"I won't keep you in suspense." Nat clutched the microphone in one hand, while sliding her finger beneath the seal of the envelope.

"Your Reunion Prom King is Jack Carter."

Everyone went wild, whistling, clapping, and chanting Jack's name. For a minute, he stood frozen to the spot. Kevin and a few of the guys nearby pushed him towards the stage.

I was probably one of the only people who didn't clap. It wasn't because I didn't want him to be the Reunion Prom King; it was because I knew he didn't care about receiving a crown from a bunch of people who hadn't been his friends.

When Jack finally made it on stage, Nat wasted no time in announcing his Queen.

"Your Reunion Prom Queen is Madison Grace."

What?

Had someone stuffed the ballot box? There was no way I'd been voted Prom Queen. I didn't want to go up there.

Noreen's judgy gaze was drilling a hole in me. She certainly wasn't happy, wasn't clapping, and was probably wondering if I'd stuffed the ballot box.

Elise came out of nowhere. "Congratulations, Madison. Go up there and get your crown." She smiled and applauded.

I swallowed and slowly walked towards the stage. When I got closer, I finally glanced up. Jack was watching me. I wasn't sure what he was thinking or if he was still upset with me, and then he smiled, and I knew it was just for me, because we both knew how absurd this moment was.

A lopsided grin took over my face. When I got up on stage I stood next to him.

Nat was saying something to the crowd, so I took the opportunity to discreetly lean over to Jack. "I'm sorry."

In my periphery, I saw his smile grow even wider. He reached out and took my hand in his. I looked down at our clasped hands and up at him. Before either of us could say anything, Nat came to stand in front of us. She now had a helper on the stage with her who carried the crowns around on a pillow.

They really were doing the most with this whole Prom King and Queen thing. I tried to suppress my giggles as Nat lifted the crown from the pillow and put it on top of my head, trying to be careful not to mess up my hair. She saw the look on my face and nearly laughed herself.

"Stop," she whispered, before moving to place the crown on Jack's head. He had to stoop so she could sit it on his head.

Once Nat turned back to introduce us to the crowd as their King and Queen, Jack and I both looked at each other.

"Wanna get out of here?" I asked him.

"Hell yeah."

ELEVEN

JACK

Both Maddie and I still sported our crowns when we walked into the Drunken Yeti. It was one of the only bars in town and a hole in the wall, but way better than staying another minute at the reunion.

The minute someone recognized me, people swarmed us wanting an autograph or selfie. Being the sweetheart that she is, Maddie offered to take some of the photos. Her smiling eyes teased me while she giggled and gave orders.

I was feeling in such a good mood, I yelled across the bar. "Bartender... drinks are on me." The whole place cheered and went wild, and one of the waitresses turned to "Let's Party Every Night" on whatever music subscription service they used. I shook my head and laughed.

Once all the customers had been sufficiently satisfied with their autographs, pictures, and free alcohol, Maddie and I found a secluded spot towards the back and dropped into the red vinyl covered booth.

"I was going to buy you a drink, but I guess I owe you one." She snickered at me and plucked off her crown and set it on the table.

"I will collect," I reassured her. I meant more than just the drink. If she picked up on my innuendo, she didn't acknowledge it.

My song continued to blare loudly from the speakers. Some of the patrons were even singing along.

Maddie smiled broadly. "I told you everyone loves this song."

"Are you finally going to be honest with me and tell me you've been to one of my concerts?" I stared at her pointedly, still expecting her to elude the truth once again. My attempt at trying to be commanding was thwarted by the grin that made the corners of my mouth twitch.

The loud guffaw that she gave in answer made me laugh too. It felt like she was finally letting her guard down.

"C'mon. You can tell me," I cajoled.

Her laughter was subsiding. She bit her lip while peering at me. I could see that brain of hers trying to decide whether to lie or give me the truth.

"I've been to six of your concerts," Maddie blurted. "I even bought a t-shirt at one of them." The way she quickly added the last part was so damn cute.

"Six?" I held up six fingers and gaped at her in surprise. That was more than I expected. I'd had a sneaking suspicion that she'd at least been to one. Six shocked me.

She covered her face with her hand and nodded. I reached over and pried her fingers away from her face, but she put her other hand up in its place.

"Why are you embarrassed?" I chuckled.

Maddie turned away again and giggled while she tried to avoid my gaze.

"I promise I won't tease you. I won't even gloat."

She looked at me between her fingers in disbelief.

"Okay. I won't gloat a lot... Maddie girl, you attended six of my concerts, and you bought a t-shirt?" Every time I thought about her out in the crowd, clapping and singing along, my grin got bigger and toothier. It reminded me of how she used to attend all of my gigs back in high school.

Then I thought about the fact that not once had she tried to get backstage, see me, or tell me she saw the show and enjoyed it.

"Maddie..."

She must have heard the serious tone in my voice, because her hand dropped to her lap and the smile was wiped from her face. I still had her other hand between my own.

"Why didn't you ever try and come backstage after one of the shows?"

She swallowed but didn't offer an explanation. So I kept talking.

"You were still speaking to Austin. You could have gotten my number and called me, and we could have met up somewhere before or after." My mind went through all the possibilities.

For a moment, we both stared at each other.

"Let's not ruin the night with talking about the past. We both know why I didn't do any of those things." Her eyes pleaded with me to let it go.

I considered what she said and nodded. She was right. If I kept dredging up old wounds, we wouldn't be able to move forward. The last thing I wanted was for Maddie to get skittish about the two of us, especially when it seemed like she might be coming around to giving us a second chance.

"How about that drink?" I looked towards the bar and motioned for a waitress, hoping to lighten the mood once more. I'd be breaking my rule about only having one drink in public, but she was worth it.

A couple hours and a few drinks later, Maddie and I were

laughing about some of what happened tonight at the reunion. She laughed easily and seemed uninhibited, so I knew she was tipsy.

"Can you believe we were made prom king and queen, the two misfits?" She rubbed her fingers against the metal of the tiara, while giving it a self-deprecating look.

I couldn't take my eyes off of her. "Do you remember prom?"

The corners of her mouth tilted upwards, and I was sure she was reliving that night, before her gaze flicked up to meet mine. "Yeah... I remember prom." Her look turned coy.

That look made me wonder if she was thinking about the same part of prom night I was. "Oh yeah? What exactly do you remember?"

Beneath the table her leg brushed mine.

"Everything."

Our gazes met and held for long seconds. I was horny as hell and wanted Maddie bad. I wasn't sure whether to attribute the identical look I saw in her eyes to the liquor or to her actual feelings. As much as I wanted her, I wouldn't take advantage of her.

"Maddie girl, I think you've had enough for tonight. Why don't we head back to the cabin? It's getting late."

When she poked out her lip and proceeded to pout, all I could think about was sucking on her bottom lip.

"You're no fun." Beyond that statement, she did not put up a fuss.

I flagged down the waitress again and handed her my credit card to take care of the large tab I was sure I'd racked up.

After the waitress brought my card back along with the receipt, I signed it and left her a handsome tip. Before she could walk away, I stopped her. "Is it okay if I leave the car in the lot and have it picked up in the morning?" Even though I didn't feel buzzed, there was no way I would get behind the wheel, and I definitely wasn't going to let Maddie drive.

"Of course. No one will mess with it." She smiled. "Would you like me to call you a cab?"

"That would be great... Also, can I leave the key with you for my brother. He'll be the one to pick it up."

"Austin." She said his name without the hint of a question. The fact that she knew who my brother was without me having to tell her briefly made me wonder how often Austin had to deal with people impeding on his life because we were related.

"Yep. That's him." I picked the keys up from the table and made sure I had my cabin key and that Maddie's wasn't attached before I handed them to her.

"I'll make a note in case I'm not the one here when he comes by." The waitress took the keys and the signed receipt and walked away. I texted my brother a message about the car knowing he would get it back to the cabin the minute he got up.

Maddie let me help her into her jacket, and then we stepped outside into the cold night air. It was a beautiful night. The stars twinkled in the sky, and the smell of pine scented the air. Maddie shivered and leaned into me, resting her head against my chest. Her hair smelled like coconut and vanilla. I wondered if her body would smell that way, and all I could envision was licking her. I settled for wrapping my arms around her. We stayed like that until the cab arrived.

In the back seat, she rested her head on my shoulder. I gave the driver our destination and he pulled off. It was too dark for him to make out who I was, so thankfully we had a quiet ride.

She never let go of my arm when we exited the cab and climbed the steps to the cabin. When we entered, I turned on the lamp. It gave the room a warm glow.

Maddie walked into the middle of the living room and tossed her purse and crown onto one of the armchairs, where they landed haphazardly. I watched her while she pulled off her coat and sent it sailing onto the chair with the rest of her things.

With a flirtatious look in her eyes, she strutted towards me. Something electric leapt between us, but I wasn't sure what it was. Anticipation filled the air.

Maddie reached up and took the crown off my head. I'd forgotten I was still wearing the damned thing. She tossed it onto the sofa and looked up at me, those luscious brown eyes filled with want and need. The last thing I wanted was to take advantage of her and have her regret things tomorrow.

She placed her hands on my shirt and moved them beneath my jacket until she was pushing the garment off my shoulders.

"You're drunk. Maybe we shouldn't do this?" Those were the words that came out of my mouth, but my body was saying an entirely different thing. I was trying really hard to be the gentleman, but I wanted to rip Maddie's clothes off, bend her over the sofa, fuck her, and then spend the rest of the night making love to her until we were both sweaty and exhausted.

My jacket fell to the floor in a heap at our feet.

"I'm not that drunk." Maddie's gaze stayed locked on mine, and she reached for me, twining her arms around my neck.

Out of reflex, my arms wound themselves around her waist, and I pulled her closer, eliminating any space between us. This close, she could feel the lie I told her and myself.

"I just don't want you to regret anything in the morning." There I was, still trying to be chivalrous, even though she was now pulling my face down to meet hers.

"The only thing I'll regret in the morning is if you're not in my bed."

The tempting little seductress said those words and then kissed me like she was trying to steal my breath.

I took control, mastering her until she whimpered in compliance. Cradling her head in my hands, my tongue invaded the sweetness of her mouth. Maddie tasted of the fruity martinis she'd ordered throughout the night.

While we kissed, we stumbled our way to the bedrooms. In the hallway, standing between the two rooms, still lip-locked, I finally came up for air.

"Which room," I panted.

She pointed to her bedroom and we resumed pawing and kissing as we entered. I kicked the door closed with my foot. Moonlight streamed in through the windows, bathing us in its glow. I paused again and cupped her face in my hands. "Are you sure?" I wanted to give her one final out.

"Make love to me, Jack." The sweet plea was said without hesitation.

That was all I needed. I was going to do more than make love to Maddie. My mouth crashed into hers again, and I kissed the life out of her. The animal in me wanted to rip that dress off her curvaceous body, but I knew better than to ruin a woman's clothes. If it were her panties, I would have ripped those suckers off her with no problem, but there was no way I was going to ruin her dress.

"How do I get this thing off of you?" My hands were already skimming her breasts, hips, and back as I searched for an opening, buttons, or a zipper. I was impatient to feel her bare skin beneath my hands. A few seconds ticked by, and my brain would no longer consider preserving her dress.

When I pulled the dress over her head I heard a ripping sound, and I was pretty certain a button dropped onto the floor.

"I'll buy you another one," I said hastily.

Giggles shook Maddie's body while she stood before me, still wearing her tights, a thong, her boots, and something else I couldn't take my eyes off of.

It looked like wings were covering her breasts. There were no straps or band. She undid some string in between her cleavage that was holding it together and then peeled the wings from her skin. The minute the interesting item came off, I no longer cared to know what the thing was called. My eyes were riveted on her perky, round globes. Her nipples stood at attention after being uncovered.

"You're perfect," I uttered while reaching to cup her breasts in the palms of my hands. My thumbs rubbed across her nipples. A small gasp fell from Maddie's lips and I wanted to hear more of those delicious sounds.

I bent my head and sucked one of her nipples into my mouth. She rewarded me with crying out, and she pulled my head into her bosom. It was evident she was enjoying the sensations my tongue and mouth created. I gathered her closer and continued to devour her flesh. After a few minutes I switched to the other nipple, suckling it into my mouth, wanting to give them equal attention. I laved the nub with my tongue and closed my eyes while savoring her flesh.

Once I released her, her hands were everywhere, on my belt buckle, on the buttons of my shirt. The next thing I knew, buttons went flying everywhere when Maddie ripped my shirt open.

"I'll buy you another one." She winked at me, while wearing the sexiest smirk I'd ever seen on her. I grinned.

Both of us worked frantically to get the shirt down my arms and off my body. Then she resumed the work on my belt buckle. While she was busy with that, I pulled her close and dropped open mouth kisses onto her neck and shoulder.

My belt buckle clattered against the floor, and cool air kissed the skin on my legs when she pushed my pants down. I toed off my shoes and then released her so I could tug my pants off.

I pushed Maddie down on the edge of the bed and knelt before her. A hungry look was in my eyes when I peered at her.

She was gorgeous. I ran my hands down the sides of her legs and watched her breath hitch in her throat at my touch. When I caressed her left calf and lifted it, Maddie leaned back on her palms and watched me under hooded eyes.

Without breaking eye contact, I pulled her ankle boot off and tossed it over my shoulder. It landed with a thud. Gently, I kissed her instep and then placed her foot on the floor. I repeated the gesture, caressing her right calf and lifting her leg to remove her other shoe.

My dick was getting hard just thinking of all the things I planned to do to her. I sat her foot on the ground and then pushed her to lie back on the bed. She leaned up on her elbows so she could continue to watch me. I gave her a smirk and put my fingers into the top of her tights and pulled them down her hips and off her legs. After feathering kisses across her painted toes, I ran my hands up from her ankles, back to her waist.

Her eyes were clouded with lust, and I was sure my own matched. I could smell her. I nuzzled the small piece of fabric that covered her nether lips. Her breathless moan egged me on, and I swiped my tongue across the silk, making her wriggle beneath me. I wanted more. I needed the taste of her.

Leaning back, I gripped her thong and slid it from her body. The minute that was out of the way, I pulled her hips to the edge of the bed and pushed her legs open so I could look at her.

My fingers stroked her folds, and then I pushed two of them inside of her heat and found her wet. After moving them in and out of her a few times, I pulled them out and rubbed the dewiness between my fingers. "You're so wet." I looked up at her. Maddie was watching me, her mouth parted.

I licked the taste of her from my fingers. My eyes shut for the briefest moment while I savored her. When I opened them, she was still staring at me. Her eyes even more sex starved, if that was possible.

"I'm going to enjoy you." I made the promise right before I placed her knees over my shoulders and stuck my tongue deep in her slick channel.

Her back arched off the bed, and instantly her fingers were in my hair, pulling and pushing me deeper into her core.

Maddie repeated the word "yes" several times. The minute I had a taste, I planned to feast on her as much as I could. She tasted like ambrosia. Even as I partook of her sweetness, all I could think was that I wanted more. I closed my eyes and ate her like a death row inmate enjoying his last meal. She squirmed and groaned beneath my mouth. I locked my arms and hands around her thighs tighter to hold her still. When she came I was going to get every drop of her sweet nectar.

Minutes later, when her thighs began to quiver and shake, I knew she was going to come soon. My thumb strummed her sensitive little nub like I was playing a song. In no time, her back bowed, and she yelled my name. "Jack!"

Maddie came good and hard, and I lapped it up.

When I finally unlatched my mouth from her goodness, I swiped my hand across my wet mouth. She lay on the bed staring up at me, while trying to catch her breath. A tiny tremor ran through her as she came down from her climax, and she shivered.

My boxer briefs were now the last barrier between us. I stood and shoved them down my legs and kicked them away.

Thankfully, my brain wasn't so far gone in its quest to be inside of her. I remembered I needed to get the condom from my wallet. Not sure if she was thinking straight, coming off the high of her orgasm, but I wouldn't go bareback without her permission. I yanked my pants from the floor and pulled my wallet out. With a speed I wasn't aware I was capable of, I found the condom, ripped that sucker open and eased it onto my throbbing dick.

Maddie watched me, while she scooted to the top of the bed, not stopping until her head hit the pillow. I climbed onto the mattress and positioned myself between her thighs. Our naked bodies touched and my skin felt like it would go up in flames. My dick pulsed against her wet opening. I looked down between our bodies and took hold of my dick in my hand, lining it up with her entrance. Her thighs cradled me.

I looked back up at her before I plunged deep inside of her. Both of us gasped loudly. Once I was balls deep, I halted any movement, giving her body time to adjust to my invasion. She wrapped her legs around me, crossing her ankles, and hooked her arms underneath mine. When she rolled her hips, I knew she was giving me the go ahead.

Once she did that, I didn't have to be told twice. I pulled out and then slowly pushed back in, grinding against her the instant I was fully seated inside of her once more. The low moans that came from her turned me on even further.

Memories of our first night together filled me for a second, and I was reminded of trying to coax her to be more vocal. Gone was the timid lover she'd been. Her nails scratched my back while she moved with my body. I knew it was only experience that could have turned her into the amazing lover she was, and I became determined to drive any other man from her memory.

I was going to stamp my damn mark all over that woman. Every inch of skin, inside and out, would say "Jack Carter."

With those thoughts I began to thrust harder and deeper. Maddie cried out, "More."

Hell yes.

I'd give my woman all she could take, and then some. Once I started fucking her even faster, I knew I was hitting that spot because she ceased to use words, instead groaning and panting. Sweat dripped from us, and the air was pungent with sex. I knew she was close by the way her wetness sucked me in even further every time I drove into her.

"Come for me, Maddie girl..." The words came out strained as I tried to hold on to some semblance of control. She had to get hers before I got mine. I reached my hand between us and rubbed that little bundle of nerves, knowing it would drive her over the edge.

"Yes," She keened right before she detonated. Watching her climax, and feeling her pulse and throb with the orgasm that shook her body made me drive into her at an erratic pace. I was a wild man as I felt my own impending orgasm looming. I wanted to prolong it, but her greedy core was having none of it. It pulled the orgasm from my body. Her channel clenched my dick, milking it of every drop.

"Fuck," I grunted. I emptied my seed into the condom.

I rolled to my side, taking her with me so I wouldn't put my weight on her. Even though I was slightly out of breath, I pulled her close and kissed her, while I slowly pumped into her a few more times. My dick couldn't seem to get enough of her. Finally, I pulled out and broke our kiss. I got up from the bed and headed into the bathroom where I pulled the condom off and tied it off before dropping it into the trashcan.

When I rejoined her in the bed, it wasn't too much time later that we began round two. This time I made slow, sweet love to Maddie before she fell asleep in my arms.

TWELVE

MADDIE

True to my word, there was nothing I regretted about last night. The first time Jack and I slept together was after prom, in a hotel room here at Holiday Springs Resort. The last time we slept together was that summer after graduation, shortly before we broke up. Teenage Jack had been a good lover to an inexperienced girl, but grown-ass Jack had me forgetting my damn name last night.

The grin would not leave my face. Even though I had a slight ache between my legs, I didn't care.

"What are you thinking about, Maddie girl?" The low rumble of his voice, still tinged with sleep, made my heart beat a little faster.

My face grew heated and flushed at being caught grinning like a fool, while I thought about the things he'd done to me last night.

"Nothing." I smiled coyly.

"Oh no. You were thinking about something." Jack reached over and began tickling my sides.

I squealed and giggled and tried to push his hands away.

"Tell me." He laughed, his eyes crinkling at the corners. Hoping to get me to confess, he continued tickling me.

"Okay, okay." I panted, trying to catch my breath.

"I was thinking about... I was thinking about... the way your eyes looked when you saw my bra last night." I lied through my teeth, and he knew it, but we both fell back on the bed, chuckling.

"Liar," Jack teased me, while pulling me into his side. He dropped a kiss on the top of my head.

Before I could stop myself, I let out a sigh. I held my breath waiting to see what he would do. When he squeezed me and seemed to hold me a bit tighter, I knew without looking at his face that he was smiling. I knew it wasn't the kind of smug, self-satisfied smile that some men would be sporting right about now knowing they'd satisfied their woman. Not Jack, he'd be wearing the smile of a man that hoped this moment, this feeling lasted forever. I felt the same way.

"How about we take a nice long shower together..." He rubbed his hand down my back and cupped my ass in his hand. "Afterwards, I'll make us breakfast, we skip the rest of the reunion stuff and find some activity at the lodge to do... just me and you?"

The question in his tone at the end made me smile. Even after last night, part of him was still unsure of my feelings.

I leaned up on my elbow and peered at him. "There's nothing I'd love more than to spend the day with you, Jack Carter."

He sat up, pulling me with him, and cupped my face in his hands. If it were possible for a kiss to be equal parts sexy and sweet, Jack managed it with the delivery of his kiss. When he pulled away, I licked my bottom lip, relishing the taste of him.

"Let's take that shower." The huskiness in his voice told me we were going to get really dirty in that shower.

Just as I suspected we would, we went at it in the shower like our bodies were ravenous wolves. It was like we'd been starving for each other these last ten years.

Jack pinned me against the wall and while his dick was busy making me see stars, his mouth licked and sucked every inch of my flesh it could reach. By the time we emerged, we were a little pruney, and the morning had slipped into the afternoon.

After we dressed, I sat in the kitchen talking to Jack while he cooked. Things were more relaxed between us than they'd been since high school. I cracked up while he told me funny stories of touring with his band. At one point he checked his text messages.

"Austin dropped your car off this morning. He said he put the keys in the mailbox."

I hadn't even thought about the car, but was grateful he'd been thinking for both of us last night.

As we ate, we looked over some of the resort activity brochures that were left on the table for guests.

"What about the sleigh ride?" Jack passed me the brochure and then bit into his toast. He chewed and swallowed before resuming his endorsement for the activity. "We can ride around and..."

"Admire nature." I interrupted him.

"The only thing I plan on admiring is you, Maddie girl."

I'd forgotten what hearing him call me that did to me. My insides literally melted to goop when he said that and looked at me the way he was doing now. His eyes drank me in, devouring me with a hungry intensity. We stared into each other's eyes. There was a part of me that wanted to take him back to bed and stay there all day. The other part of me was looking forward to a day of romance.

Jack grinned and continued. "We can snuggle beneath the

blanket. We can drink hot cider, and I can come up with other ways to keep you warm."

My cheeks got warm at his words. "We're not going to be alone." I bit my lip and tried not to show any interest in what his plans might be.

"The driver won't be able to see us. He's going to be facing the opposite direction, plus we'll have the blanket to cover our dirty deeds." He waggled his eyebrows at me. "Part of the fun is hoping we get caught." Beneath the table he massaged my knee, and warmth spread throughout my body. Again I considered staying in the cabin.

"Okay, sleigh ride it is."

He clapped his hands together and leaned across the table and kissed me.

After we cleaned up together, we put on our coats, scarves, gloves and hats and headed out. On our walk to the main lodge, we held hands. I was okay with the silence.

"Wait a second, I think I dropped something." Jack let go of my hand to stoop and pick up whatever it was.

I moved ahead of him while I watched some kids build a snowman at one of the passing cabins.

"Maddie?"

"Hmm?" I turned to see what Jack wanted, and that's when something cold, and wet whizzed through the air and struck me in the chest.

My mouth fell open in surprise. I didn't even try to suppress the grin and then the laugh that bubbled up. "You punk." I dropped to the ground and formed a lumpy snowball and pitched it at him. It hit him on the shoulder.

"It's on."

Suddenly, we were both ducking and dodging the snowballs that we lobbed at each other. I could barely aim properly, because my giggling kept making me inept. Jack's snowballs nailed me every time, which only made things more comical in my eyes.

Several minutes passed in our snowball war before Jack ran up and tackled me into a pile of snow. By that point, I was laughing so hard my sides ached. Even though I was wearing a hat, the ends of my hair weren't covered. The back of my hair was getting wet and curling the longer I lay in the ice. For a Black woman with a relaxer, in any other situation I'd be pissed right about now, but I didn't care. That's how much Jack had gotten under my skin: that I didn't care my hair was being ruined.

He lay on top of me, his eyes full of mischief, before he leaned down and gave me a slow, sweet kiss. Before things could get out of hand, I reluctantly pushed against his chest.

"We better keep it PG. There are kids nearby." I giggled. "Plus, I'm cold. My butt's getting numb." We both laughed at that.

Jack stood and reached out his hand to help me up. He pulled me into his body. His large hand covered my ass, massaging. "Do you feel that?" Considering his hard-on was pressed against my belly, I wasn't sure if he meant that or the pleasurable sensations his hand was creating in my backside. I simply nodded, too tongue-tied for a verbal response. When he removed his hand from my ass, he took my hand in his, and we continued on to the lodge.

Before we could get to the entrance of the lodge, I noticed the lake and then the outdoor ice rink. Even though it was daytime, the surrounding trees and wooden slatted fence were covered in glowing twinkle lights.

In all the time I'd lived in New York City, I'd yet to visit the ice-skating rink that Rockefeller Center opened up every winter. Always too busy with work. Seeing the rink here at

Holiday Springs reminded me of the long-ago dates with Jack out on the ice, holding hands.

I tugged on Jack's arm. "Hey. Let's go ice skating before the sleigh ride."

He looked towards the rink and then back at me. "You sure you remember how to put two feet in front of the other on a pair of blades." His eyes crinkled at the edges when he gave me a teasing smile.

"I bet I'm better than you."

JACK

Within a couple minutes of being on the ice, I bit it hard and landed flat on my ass. Maddie bathed me in her adorable giggles. A young kid skated by looking like she was ready to launch into a triple salchow, while Maddie clutched her stomach, doubled over in laughter, maintaining perfect balance on her skates.

"It looks like you should have been worried about yourself on those skates." She reached out a hand to help me up.

I was tempted to pull her down next to me on the cold ice. Instead, I took her hand and got back on my feet. "I guess it's been a while."

"Mmmhmm." Maddie giggled and took my hand in hers.

I was shaky at first when we resumed skating, but after a couple more laps, I began to feel a little more sure-footed. Again, memories of the past flooded my mind. The last thing I wanted to do was keep reliving the past, but I couldn't help myself. I was holding my Maddie girl again, and I was ready to make a whole lot of new memories with her, that was for damn sure.

"What are you thinking about?"

She broke me from my thoughts. Those inquisitive brown eyes gazed at me. Part of me wanted to pour out my heart, but I found myself holding back. What if she was just having fun? What if she didn't mean for this to go beyond the week? I didn't want to spoil the day, because we were having a great time together, but I knew at some point we needed to have a serious conversation, because I wanted more than just today or tomorrow, I wanted forever.

"Just concentrating on staying upright." I grinned at her.

The sound of our skates cutting through the ice filled the silence that followed. It wasn't terribly crowded. People were scattered across the rink: families, couples, clusters of teenagers. A few people had looked in our direction, but none had approached me for autographs or pictures which I was thankful for. I simply wanted to spend time with Maddie.

"Did you ever imagine that this would happen?"

I looked at her slightly puzzled. "What do you mean?"

Maddie looked up at me. "This." She raised our conjoined hands slightly. "Us... That we would... that we would..." It was clear she was searching for the right words to try and categorize exactly what we were.

Her question caught me off guard. So, she was thinking about things between us as well. It was a welcome change from how much time she spent running away from what was happening between us.

"No, I didn't think this would happen, but I'm glad it did." I squeezed her hand.

The smile she gifted me with made me feel like I was walking on clouds. She leaned into me and we continued to skate.

"Do you think Nat is pissed we didn't show up for anymore of the reunion activities?" Maddie chuckled.

"She'll get over it. She's your best friend. I'm sure she'll forgive you. If not, there's always bribery. We can get her something nice and expensive." My joke made Maddie laugh harder.

Neither of us wanted to be at another awful reunion event, talking to people that hadn't cared about us then or now. Maybe later, we could get together with Nat and Kevin. Thinking about Nat and Kevin, and our long friendship with them. Back in the day, those two were usually around when Maddie would challenge me in a race or any number of things. I was reminded of the challenge she threw at me earlier when we decided to come to the rink.

"I remember you saying you were better than me? Now that my muscle memory has kicked in, care to race?" I tried not to smirk when I looked at her, knowing she'd be unable to say no.

"Okay." The impish grin she gave me was adorable.

"Let's make it more interesting. A little wager?"

Maddie's eyes sparkled in amusement and she dropped my hand to turn and skate backwards, so she was now facing me. "What's the wager?" She crossed her arms over her chest and arched a brow at me.

"If I win, you owe me a striptease, complete with a lap dance." I was practically drooling thinking of that plump ass of hers in some sexy lingerie, gyrating and shaking those hips while she straddled me. I fully expected her to protest.

"Okay. If I win, you owe me a lap dance."

Boy, I'd missed this woman.

"Maddie girl, if you win, I will give you the best lap dance you ever had."

Without another word, she turned away from me and began sprinting away on her ice skates.

"Go." She shouted over her shoulder, while laughing.

"You little cheat." I shouted and gave chase, unable to stop laughing myself.

While I had grown accustomed to being on skates again, it

was clear that Maddie was a more skilled skater than I was. She cut through the crowd with grace. I was a big, clumsy oaf, barely missing knocking women and children over trying to get past her. There was no way she hadn't been ice skating regularly?

Up ahead Maddie glided to a stop near the wall. She turned and raised her arms over her head in victory. "I won."

Seconds later, I reached her and instead of coming up beside her, I skated up to her and placed my hands on the wall on either side of her, caging her in.

We gazed into each other's eyes.

"I won." She said the words softly while sporting a Cheshire cat grin.

"Looks like someone's getting a lap dance tonight." I pressed my body into hers, our lips mere inches from each other.

"I'm expecting the full Magic Mike experience, Jack."

I had been about to kiss her, but the minute she said that I guffawed and rested my forehead against hers. She had such a great sense of humor.

"I mean it. I expect a great show." Maddie was doing her best to suppress her laughter.

"Anything for you." I pulled back and cupped her face in my hands. Briefly, I gazed into her eyes before I kissed her senseless.

When I pulled away moments later, she wore a dazed expression.

"Why don't we go see about that sleigh ride. I want to be alone with you." My heated gaze let her know exactly what I had planned for her.

"We're not going to be alone. There will be someone driving the sleigh." She swallowed when she realized the hungry look in my eyes didn't disappear.

"In the back of the sleigh, with the driver's back to us, it will just be the two of us." If Maddie thought the presence of a driver who wouldn't be able to see us was going to deter me from doing wicked things to her, she was mistaken.

I took her hand and led her off the ice. Once I helped her take her skates off, I removed my own and we turned them at the counter and headed to the lodge.

FOURTEEN

MADDIE

We entered the lodge through the back and headed to guest services to find out if we would be able to go out on a sleigh ride, despite not having a reservation. Thankfully, there was availability to go out immediately.

It was a short walk to the stables. When we arrived, we were greeted by the sleigh driver.

"I'm Chapman. How are you both doing today?" Chapman greeted us, shaking Jack's hand, then mine.

"We're doing well. I'm Jack. This is Maddie." Jack said.

Then I chimed in like we were some old married couple. "Just wanted to enjoy a scenic ride around the resort." I looked around the wooded area outside the barn and stables. "How many rides have you given today?"

"Believe it or not, you're our first guests today. Henrietta and Heidi will be excited to leave the stable and get some exercise."

"Are those the horses?" I pointed towards two large, beautiful horses with silky manes, that stood nearby, munching on hay.

Chapman looked towards the horses and gave them a fond

smile. "Yep." He turned back to us. "Well, go ahead and make yourselves cozy in the sleigh."

Jack helped me climb into the back of the sleigh, which looked like the carriage I remembered them using in the summers. The seat was a comfy looking, black leather bench seat with a padded back.

Chapman handed us a wool blanket. "Would you prefer cider or hot chocolate?"

I glanced at Jack, trying to see if he had a preference. He must have read something in my expression, because he turned to Chapman and answered without asking me. "Bring us one of each. We'll share."

It made me smile that he knew me so well, because that's exactly what I was going to suggest.

First, Chapman hitched the horses to the sleigh. Then he entered another building off the stables, which was probably where he would prepare our beverages.

Once we were settled in, Jack arranged the heavy fur-lined blanket across our lap. Beneath the blanket, he squeezed my thigh. I knew what he had on his mind. Smirking, I grabbed his hand and placed it on his thigh.

"We haven't even left the stable yet," I whispered. The thrill of being caught like a pair of horny teenagers kind of turned me on, but the modest part of me pulled on the reins.

Jack snickered but behaved himself. A few minutes later, Chapman returned and handed up the disposable cups covered with lids, before he took his seat at the front of the carriage.

While we waited on the hot liquid to cool off, we made polite conversation with Chapman. When I felt like the hot chocolate was okay to drink without scalding my tongue, I took a sip and snuggled into Jack's side. It was such a perfect moment. The land was blanketed in pristine white snow. The branches on the trees were even snow covered.

We fell into a silence and just enjoyed nature unfolding in its beauty all around us. An area of the trail ran through the woods without cabins lined around. Discreetly, Jack took my cup from my hand and placed it in one of the cup holders. I didn't try to stop him. The mischief and lust that mingled on his face excited me. Underneath the blanket, his hand slid into my lap. He cupped my heat between his hands. I pursed my lips together to keep from sighing out loud and giving us away.

When he reached up and undid the button on my jeans, I looked at him in shock. Jack put his finger to his lips, the ghost of a grin lurking just beneath the surface. Slowly, he slid down my zipper, making sure the noise was minimal and eaten up by the noise of the horse's hooves hitting the ground.

My body wanted whatever he had planned, because I found myself adjusting my position so he would have more room when he slid his hand into my pants, which I was sure was his plan. The whole time he tortured me and made me wait, I couldn't take my eyes off the back of Chapman's head. I was waiting for the man to whip around and say, "Gotcha."

Finally, Jack slid his hand into the waistband of my underwear. I inhaled sharply at his contact with my skin. He'd removed his glove and his fingers were cold. They found their way to my folds and began to rub back and forth. I became lost in the ecstasy he made me feel. When he slipped a digit inside of me, I clapped my hand over my mouth, afraid I would moan out loud.

"You're so fucking sexy, trying to stay silent." His voice was low and full of need.

I put my hand in his lap and rubbed his hard on. The hand that wasn't stuffed down my pants grabbed it and put it back in my lap. "This isn't about me. This is about your pleasure right now," he whispered before licking my earlobe.

Soon I was so far gone and couldn't stop myself from undulating my hips and grinding down on his finger.

Jack watching me turned me on even further as I rode his finger. Once he started rubbing my bud while pushing his finger in and out of my slick heat, I knew it wouldn't be long before I came.

Just when I could feel myself unraveling do to the swift climax that was coming, Jack leaned over and planted his lips on mine, taking my soft moans into his mouth. He continued pumping his finger in and out of my wetness, while my body quaked. It wasn't until I squirmed and pushed at his hand that he let up. I was so sensitive to the touch, even my panties rubbing against my skin made me shiver.

Jack pulled back and stuck his fingers in his mouth, continuing to stare into my eyes while he sucked on his fingers, enjoying the taste of me. After a few minutes, I zipped up my pants and buttoned them. I didn't need to look over to know that Jack was sporting a smile while he tugged his glove back on.

Of course, now that it was over, all I could think about was whether Chapman knew what was going on in the back of his sleigh. Jack handed me my cup, which was still surprisingly warm, and I leaned into him and drank my hot chocolate. I was sated and a little drowsy after my orgasm.

We were out for about another forty-five minutes before we returned to the stable. Jack climbed down first and then helped me down.

"Thank you," Jack said and reached for his wallet. He pulled out several bills and handed them to Chapman.

The man graciously accepted, and we headed back to the lodge. My hand was tucked into his as we walked the trail.

"Today has been one of the best days I've had in a long time that didn't have anything to do with my music." Jack looked down at me.

"Me too," I said softly. It was true. Waking up with him and everything that came after had been so perfect and wonderful. Not once had I thought about work or checking my email. I was consumed with him, and I was okay with that. I was a little scared of what my heart felt. Jack and I had only just reentered each other's lives after a long absence. Was it too soon to be making plans for a future? Or did we both just know?

Jack hadn't taken his eyes off me. He brought our entwined hands up to his lips and placed a kiss on the back of my hand. "I need to stop at the lodge and handle something. Why don't you head back to the cabin? What do you think about having dinner with Nat, Kevin, and Austin tonight? Then later tonight, I can make love to you in front of a warm fire." He teased me, knowing when he talked like that in public I got a little bashful, wondering if people overheard or knew the things he was saying to me.

"That sounds like the perfect ending to this perfect day."

Outside the lodge, we stood kissing like we were going to be parted longer than the time it would take him at the lodge. I'm sure we both should have cared about someone taking pictures of us, since Jack had the tabloids to worry about, but neither of us was concerned. When he finally pulled away, I licked my bottom lip and smiled. "I'll see you back at the cabin."

On the trail back, I couldn't stop reflecting on everything that had taken place between us over the past several days. Never had I thought, when I showed up for the reunion, that I could end up giving Jack a second chance. I was feeling like I was walking on a cloud, which was very unlike me. I was usually pretty grounded, but I had butterflies in my stomach. I was rocking the rose-colored glasses with flare, and I felt like I was about to hear songbirds and start skipping.

I was so deep in my thoughts when I arrived at the cabin, I wasn't looking up.

"Do you know where Jack Carter is?"

The feminine voice made my head pop up. One look at her, and all the thoughts I'd had on the walk here, all the feelings about the day, quickly took a nosedive. I was staring at some glamazon with long, dirty blonde hair, sun-kissed skin, and gorgeous blue eyes. She looked familiar, which I was sure was because she was someone famous.

I couldn't help it. My gaze swept her from the top of her head down to the expensive designer snow boots she wore. Did she really have her midriff showing in the middle of winter? If only I was that self-assured.

Slowly, I moved up the porch steps like I was in a trance. I bit my lip to stop the quiver. Angry tears stung my eyes. I would not cry in front of one of Jack's bimbos.

"You can wait for him inside." Part of me wanted to be Petty McPetty and make her wait outside, but my mother had raised me better than that. I could hear her now if I'd left the glamazon outside to freeze to death. It didn't matter that she was my rival. I was still to be hospitable.

Not once did she ask me who I was. Or why some woman she didn't know was entering Jack's cabin with a key. Clearly, she wasn't worried about who I was to him. Maybe she was used to him having a sidepiece or dating more than one woman at a time. That wasn't the kind of woman I was. If the situation had been reversed, and I'd been waiting to surprise my boyfriend and some trollop strolled up the path with a key, the heifer would have to explain herself.

Upon entering, she glanced around the living room. "So quaint." She parked her luggage near her and sat on the sofa, relegating me to an armchair.

On the inside I raged. I'd believed him, believed every word that came out of his mouth, and the whole time he'd been playing me. I felt like a fool. I'd known he was selfish, but I didn't know he'd turned into a liar, a cheat, and an asshole. Why would he play with my heart and my emotions like that, and give me some of the best sex I'd ever had in my life? My traitorous body was still affected by the memory of his touch. I was angrier that I didn't seem to have any control over that.

Whoever she was, she was so busy checking herself out in the mirror on her compact and reapplying another coat of lip gloss that she was ignorant to my turmoil. I wanted to be angry with her, but all the animosity I felt was directed at him.

Jack Carter had broken my heart all over again.

FIFTEEN

JACK

I watched Maddie head back to the cabin. The way her ass swayed when she walked made me unable to tear my eyes away until she was out of sight.

When I walked inside, I headed to the front desk and asked for Dawson, the man who the owner had assured me could take care of anything I needed. I wanted tonight to be special. Cassie was working the front desk again when I walked up.

"Hey there, Cassie. Is Dawson around?"

The minute she looked up and saw it was me, she went all red in the face and averted her gaze. "Sure, Mr. Carter…"

"Remember, it's Jack." I corrected her. Mr. Carter made me sound like her dad. I was sure I was older than her, but not by that much.

She blushed. "Right. Let me just give him a call."

Five minutes later, Dawson walked up to the desk. "How may I help you Mr. Carter?" I didn't bother correcting him.

"I was hoping you could make some reservations for me, but also I needed some things delivered to my cabin tonight before we come back from dinner. Things to set a romantic mood."

"Whatever you need." Dawson smiled at me knowingly.

I was determined to make the ending to this day as memorable for both of us, as it could possibly be.

Once I finished going over everything I needed with Dawson, I left the lodge, eager to see Maddie's beautiful face. We'd only been apart from each other for maybe twenty or thirty minutes, but I found myself craving her company. I was glad I asked Dawson to schedule an early dinner reservation, because I planned to spend all night satisfying Maddie. It wasn't just about the sex though. It was so easy to be around her. This morning, cooking breakfast and just talking and getting reacquainted had been something I hadn't had with a woman in a long time. We could actually carry on a conversation that had nothing to do with agents, red carpets, and whether or not our picture made it into a magazine. Maddie had always been a woman of substance, and I'd missed that.

I climbed the steps to the cabin two at a time and called out her name. "Maddie girl, where you at?"

Danielle was the first thing I saw when I entered the cabin. To say I was shocked would be a grossly huge understatement. I blinked rapidly. Maybe I was imagining things. Nope. The nightmare was still seated on the sofa.

"Surprise, baby." She smiled brightly at me.

My stomach dropped. Was someone playing a cruel joke on me?

Maddie was seated on the edge of one of the large armchairs with her arms wrapped around herself. I could tell she was trying to school her features. Her fury was just barely concealed. Everything that transpired between us, all the ground that we'd covered was reversed in the space of a heartbeat. The hurt and betrayal in her eyes punched me in the gut.

"Your girlfriend came to visit." She stood and walked out of the room.

This was not good. Was that who Danielle told her she was?

I looked between Danielle and Maddie's retreating back. Even if Danielle hadn't introduced herself like that, what was Maddie supposed to think?

Danielle was about to stand, and I motioned for her to stay seated. I headed to Maddie's room and entered without knocking, shutting the door behind me. She was angrily shoving things into her suitcase.

"Maddie girl..."

Tears stood in her beautiful brown eyes when she glared at me. "Don't call me that. You don't get to call me that ever again, you filthy liar." She spit the words at me.

I sighed. "This isn't what it looks like."

She paused in her packing and snorted. "How many men have uttered that line when they've been caught cheating." She snorted. "So that woman in the living room isn't your girlfriend?"

My mind was still processing what was happening, and I took too long responding to her question. I wasn't sure what to say.

"That's what I thought." She resumed throwing things into her bag.

"Wait. Wait. You have to believe me. It isn't like that. I don't even know why she's here." Confusion clogged my brain and rendered me incapable of thinking clearly enough to say the right things that would keep Maddie here.

"It's clear to me why she's here. Surprise, baby." The last sentence mimicked Danielle's greeting to me when I entered.

"What was your plan, Jack? Get us both into bed at the same time? Or was she supposed to show up here after I was gone? After I believed that you wanted the two of us to get back together?" The more she spoke, the angrier she became until I was sure she was going to break something, given the force with which she was throwing things into her suitcase.

"Can we just talk for a second, please?" I tried to touch her.

Maddie jerked away from me. "Don't touch me." The words she flung at me were lethal and felt like arrows piercing my heart.

"Please, Maddie, let me explain. It's only you I want. I don't know why she's here." I wasn't above begging and pleading to get her to hear me out.

She finished zipping up her suitcase and pulled it off the bed. Without even looking in my direction, she stormed from the room.

I followed Maddie out into the living room and watched her walk out the front door. I wanted to run after her, to tell her that this woman meant absolutely nothing to me, tell her again that she was the only woman I wanted, until she believed it. Instead, I stood there and watched her leave.

I'd forgotten that Danielle was in the room, until I heard her in my ear. "Hey, I wanted to surprise you. Are you surprised?" She glanced out the window where I watched Maddie shove her bag in the backseat of her car. "Who was that?" Her arm snaked around my waist. She was acting like I'd called and asked her to come here. I removed her arm from my waist and stepped away.

The squeal of tires on the gravel could be heard when Maddie backed out of the driveway. When she was out of sight, my brain began to deal with my current and immediate problem.

How the fuck did Danielle find me? I knew Janine wouldn't have told her.

"What the fuck are you doing here?"

"I wanted to come see you. Didn't you miss me?" She wiggled into my side and stood on her toes to kiss me.

I both pulled away and pushed her away. "How did you find

out where I was?" I asked her again, not caring that I was blatantly hostile.

Danielle tried to look innocent, but I knew she'd done something dubious to find out exactly where I was at. The woman had the morals of a con man.

"Tell me," I demanded.

"Alright..." She let out an exaggerated sigh. "The night of your last concert I tried to get Janine to tell me where you were going, but of course she wouldn't."

Danielle huffed and rolled her eyes. "I really think you should get a new assistant, because..."

I cut off her tirade about Janine. "Just tell me how you found out." My patience was hanging on by a thin, thin thread.

She huffed again. "I was in the checkout line at the grocery store and there was a picture of you on the cover of one of those tabloids. The article mentioned that you were in your hometown and gave the name of the resort..."

I was pretty sure I knew where this was headed. It was hard to keep my cool. My hands were clenched into angry fists at my side.

"Once I looked up the resort online to get the phone number, I called and told them I was your girlfriend, but they wouldn't tell me anything. The next day when I called back, I pretended to be your mother... told them I was coming up to surprise you, and this time the person at the front desk believed my story and gave me your cabin number." She gave me a sly grin, like I should be proud of her devious tricks.

I hoped it wasn't Cassie that had fallen for that lame excuse.

"I don't know why you're so grumpy. I thought you'd be glad to see me." She invaded my personal space again, rubbing her hand up and down my chest and batting her eyes.

Without hesitating, I pushed her hand aside, and stepped back. "I was very clear the last time we saw each other that I didn't want to see you again and things were over between us."

"I thought we were just having a fight." It must have finally been sinking into Danielle's brain that she wasn't welcome here and that her feelings weren't reciprocated.

I looked at her like she had a second head. "What part of 'We're over. I never want to see you again' was unclear to you?" I threw up my hands in frustration. At this point, it didn't even matter how she came to be here. I just wanted her gone. I dropped onto the sofa.

"I know what you said, but I figured we were just taking a break." Danielle sat next to me and tried to touch my arm.

Again, I pulled away from her, growing angrier by the second. "Are you delusional? It wasn't a fight. No one was on a break. I fucking broke up with you. We haven't spoken in weeks. I don't return any of your calls. What more do you need to know it's over?" I stood. "You need to leave." I pointed at the front door.

Danielle stood and advanced towards me, still ready to make a case for whatever, I didn't care.

"Get the fuck out." I knew despite my anger that I shouldn't talk to her that way, but knowing that I may have lost Maddie for good had me seeing red.

"Grab your stuff and get out of here." I stalked towards the door and yanked it open, not caring that a rush of cold air hit me.

Danielle grabbed the handle of her roller bag and trudged towards the door. "What am I supposed to do, Jack?"

I waited until she was on the porch to answer.

"I don't know, Danielle. I didn't invite you here. Figure it out." I slammed the door in her face and locked it, then pulled out my cell phone. Frantically, I searched for Maddie's number in my phone until I realized that we had yet to swap numbers.

My finger jabbed the key for Austin's number. He picked up almost immediately.

"Hey, bro."

"What's Maddie's number?"

"Hello to you too." He said sarcastically. "Why do you need her number? Aren't you guys staying in the same place?"

I did not have time for his games. "Can you give me her number or not?" The words came out harsher than I meant them, but my patience had worn thin dealing with Danielle.

"What has you acting like an ass clown?"

"Can I please just get Maddie's number?" I was this close to ripping my brother's head off if he didn't just give me the number.

Once he gave it to me, he said one final thing. "However you screwed up, whatever you did, you better fix it." Then he hung up on me.

"Trust me. I'm trying." I mumbled to myself. I punched in the number to her phone. "Come on Maddie... pick up." Her phone rang and rang until my call was sent to voicemail.

"Damn it."

I'd never been the kind of guy who threw things or punched walls out of anger, but I was beginning to understand the unchecked aggression that coursed through you when you were extremely frustrated and upset. In that moment, I did want to upend furniture, throw something. Anything, if it helped this feeling of hopelessness go away. I knew that wasn't the answer though. After taking a deep breath, I tried Maddie's number once more. This time it went straight to voicemail.

There was only one place she could have gone: to Nat's. I couldn't call my brother again and get the number from him. I was pretty sure he wasn't going to answer after I acted like a jerk. I was about to go online when I remembered there should be some reunion newsletter in my bag that I'd stuffed in there when I was packing.

I ran to my room and rummaged around in my bag until I came up with the crinkly, glossy newsletter. Sure enough, Nat's phone number and email were on the back since she had been chairman of the reunion committee. I dialed the number. Nat picked up on the third ring.

"Hello?"

"Nat, it's Jack. Is Maddie there?" I could hear a baby crying in the background, and other children were loudly talking while a TV played.

Nat paused, and then sighed. "You know I can't tell you that."

So Maddie was there.

"I just want to talk to her," I pleaded while I paced the living room, wearing out the floorboards.

The background noises seemed to fade like Nat was heading to a quieter room.

"That's not a good idea right now." Nat was talking in a hushed whisper. "I don't know what happened between the two of you, because she won't tell me, but she was really upset when she got here." She paused. "I shouldn't even be talking to you... And I know what you're thinking Jack, but don't come here. You just need to give her time. Let her cool off. I gotta go." She hung up the phone without letting me get a word in.

I stared at my phone for a second. How long was I supposed to wait? Days ago, Austin convinced Maddie to stay for the benefit concert, which was in two days. Originally, that hadn't been her plan. What if she decided to leave sooner? I ran my hand through my hair in frustration.

I would give her the night, and then I was going to Nat's house. There was no way I would give her the opportunity to escape.

With nothing else to do and nowhere to go, I did the only thing I could do and poured myself into my music. I took out my guitar and my notepad where I wrote down lyrics and began to work on the song that had come to me that day in the bar. For now, I referred to it as Maddie's song, because she'd been the inspiration for it.

A few hours later, someone knocked on the door. I nearly tripped over my guitar case on the way to the door. Had Maddie changed her mind and decided to come back so we could talk?

A grin spread across my face before I could open the door. I deflated when I saw Dawson standing at the door instead of Maddie.

"Hey there, Mr. Carter. I thought you'd still be out to dinner. I knocked out of courtesy just in case," he said. "I have all the items you requested." He hesitated, looking past me into the living room.

"Can we come in and set it up?"

I hadn't noticed a second employee stood at the bottom of the stairs with some boxes in his hands.

"Yeah." I took a step back and opened the door wider.

The two of them carried in the ice chest, champagne, oysters, chocolate covered strawberries, extra blankets, and pillows, and set them inside the living room.

"Thanks." My words sounded hollow in my own ears. It was how I felt... hollow.

I tipped them both before they left. When they were gone, I stared at the items blankly. With everything that happened between me asking for Dawson's help and getting back here and walking into a shit storm, I'd completely forgotten about it all or I would have canceled it. Dawson looked so eager to please I didn't have the heart to tell him his efforts had been in vain. I put what I could in the refrigerator, and the perishable items that couldn't fit, I chucked in the trash. There was no way I would touch that stuff when it was intended for us together.

I went back to working on the song. Even though I knew the lonely night would only bring me dreams of her, I went to bed early so I could be at Nat's house first thing in the morning. I needed to convince her to stay. I wouldn't leave there until she agreed.

SIXTEEN

MADDIE

I was still angry with myself for believing Jack's lies when I woke up in the morning with a Lego stuck to the side of my head, after a night sleeping on Nat's sofa. My back ached, and I was groggy from the restless sleep I had.

Nat didn't tell me that he called her, but I was certain that she'd spoken to him. All I wanted to do was catch the first flight home that I could and forget this past week ever happened. Why had I ever thought coming to the reunion was a good idea? When the only vacancy was to share a cabin with Jack Carter, I should have taken any other option. But I'd made my choice, and now I'd have to live with it. Put all of it in my rearview and get back to working on making partner.

Some of Nat and Kevin's kids were already up. I could hear morning cartoons going in the other room.

What time is it?

I reached for my phone laying on the coffee table and turned it back on. While I waited for my phone to boot up, I heard Nat scold one of her kids. She was awake too. Maybe she already had some coffee brewing. I dragged myself into the kitchen clutching my phone.

She looked up when she heard me enter. "Good morning."

"Morning." I knew I looked a wreck with my swollen, red puffy eyes. My hair was probably askew because I hadn't slept on a silk pillowcase or bothered to wrap it last night. That thought reminded me how just yesterday, I'd been so head over heels for Jack that I hadn't cared if my hair had gotten wet. This morning I was cursing him because I attributed my failure to practice good hair care to him.

I padded over to her empty coffee pot. The countertop was littered with dirty dishes, cereal boxes, and other bits of things left over from the children's breakfast.

"I'm sorry, hon. If I'd known you wanted some this morning, I would have brewed a pot while I made the kids breakfast." Nat sounded so apologetic. I felt bad for springing myself on her, but knowing the city had no vacancies left me few choices. I couldn't go to Austin's because of the chance that Jack would turn up there, and the only other alternative was sleeping in my car. It was too cold for that.

I waved her off. "Please don't apologize. I should be apologizing to you. I show up unannounced in the middle of the day, teary eyed and a blubbering mess."

"You know you are welcome here anytime." She came around the island and rubbed my arm. "How are you feeling this morning?"

"Fine." She was my best friend, but I just didn't want to talk about it right now. "Where do you keep your coffee?"

Before she could answer, the doorbell rang.

"In the cupboard over there. Let me just get that. I'll be right back. Kids, you stay here and finish your breakfast."

While she went to answer her door, I opened up the cabinet she'd indicated. Relief flooded me when I spotted the canister of Folgers. The minute I picked it up, it nearly hit the roof. "No, no, no." I tore off the lid and discovered barely a handful of coffee grounds covering the bottom of the can. I put the lid back on and hung my head. Was it too much to ask for some caffeine? I groaned.

"Umm, Maddie... you have company."

When I looked up, Nat was standing in the doorway with Jack. I threw the empty container at his head without thinking. Thankfully, my aim was better than it was during our snowball fight yesterday. Jack ducked in time, missing the coffee tin that crashed into the hallway behind him.

Damn his reflexes.

"Kids... let's go upstairs and give Auntie Maddie some alone time with her guest."

Nat mouthed the word "sorry" to me before she herded her kids out of the room, and upstairs to a safer place.

Jack stepped farther into the kitchen. In the time we'd spent together at the cabin, I'd never seen him look as he did now. His appearance looked haggard. There were dark circles beneath his eyes. The rumpled clothes he wore looked like he may have slept in them.

"I deserved that, but would you just hear me out, Maddie."

He tried to come closer, and I backed around the island away from him. "You won't take my calls. I had to come... I had to come and convince you to stay."

I crossed my arms over my chest. "I want you to leave."

"Maddie, can you just hear me out? Please?" His begging was making me angrier, because a part of me wanted to hear him out, wanted to let him explain. But seeing the glamazon show up yesterday had rekindled my anger. There was no truce anymore. Her arrival had broken it.

"What do we need to discuss? You fucked me and made a fool out of me. Add another notch to your headboard. You can go back to Nashville and tell your bandmates and your friends how you spent your reunion weekend getting your kicks by getting even with your ex."

"Don't be crass." Jack scolded me like I was one of Nat's kids.

My gaze darted up to meet his, and I leveled him with a death glare.

"I'm being crass? I'm the one being crass? You're the one who had your girlfriend show up, while professing to want to be with me. Which one of us is crass, Jack?"

"I didn't ask her to come." Exasperation seeped into his words. "If you'd just hear me out, you'd know that I broke things off between us weeks ago. She's crazy."

"Why do men do that? Why does she have to be the crazy one? Are you sure you were clear with her, Jack, like you've been clear with me?" I shook my head and huffed loudly. "Why the fuck am I defending her? Now you have me defending your girlfriend. You need to go. Just go." I pointed to the front door. I just wanted him to leave.

"This was a mistake, Jack. I should have never let you back in. I blame myself." I dropped my arm to my side. Fury ravaged my body. I was so filled with it, I was shaking.

"Maddie, don't say that. Please don't say that. You don't mean it." The sadness in his voice hurt me. I knew it was my anger talking, but I wanted to hurt him as deeply as I was hurting.

"I do." I lied.

He came around the island so fast I didn't have a chance to escape.

"Please. Just listen to me." He penned me in, hands planted on the counter, on either side of me. "Please, Maddie." His tone was so plaintive, and having him this close wore down my defenses.

I didn't say anything, letting him take that as his sign that I was allowing him to plead his case.

"Thank you..."

Jack kept trying to make eye contact, but I refused to look up. My eyes stayed focused on my bare toes and the wooden floor.

"It's true what I told you... I dumped Danielle weeks ago. I told her we were over, and I never wanted to see her again. That's the truth. One of the guests or employees, hell it could have been one of our classmates from the reunion, that took my picture and sold it to a tabloid. That's how Danielle found out I was here. Then she lied to the staff to find out my cabin number. I promise you I did not ask her to come here. The minute you left the cabin, I sent her packing."

I still didn't respond or look at him.

"Please, Maddie, you have to believe me." He pressed his forehead to mine, silently pleading with me. I couldn't hold my emotions in check any longer. My anger was wearing on me. Tears streamed down my face.

"Maddie girl, don't cry. Please don't cry." His voice was filled with anguish. He reached up and attempted to wipe my tears away with the pads of his thumbs. Then he was pressing his lips to mine.

For a minute, I was lost. My lips parted, and his tongue swept inside. Why did the glamazon have to show up and ruin everything? What if she wasn't the only one, and this was just a lie to get me back into bed? How could I trust him?

I shoved against him. "No. No. Don't try and make me forget what's happened."

Jack stumbled backwards. I ran my finger across my lip and stared at him with tortured eyes. He hung his head.

"I'll go..." He looked up at me again. "I'll go if you promise me you won't leave town, that you'll stay and come to the concert. Promise me that, and I'll leave. Just say you'll come." The desperate look in his eyes made me consider his offer.

"You'll leave?"

He nodded. "I'll leave."

I peered at the wall while I thought about his proposition. "Fine. I'll stay and attend the concert." I wrapped my arms around my body, wondering if he was going to keep his promise.

"Okay then." He said the words softly. Without another word, he turned and left the kitchen. Seconds later, I heard the front door open and close.

I stayed in my position at the counter for another minute, before I crossed the room and went into the hall to retrieve the canister I'd thrown. Nat was rushing down the stairs. "Was that the door I heard? Did he leave? What happened? Are you okay?"

She peeked into the kitchen. "You didn't throw anything else did you?"

I shook my head, walked back into her kitchen, and sat the empty coffee can on the countertop.

"You're my best friend Nat, but right now I need a shower, and I need coffee. After those two things, maybe I will finally be in a state to talk about everything." I didn't wait for her response. Walking back to the living room, I grabbed a towel from my bag and went to the bathroom.

The whole time, I just kept wondering what Jack expected to happen when I showed up at the concert? I could still leave. *No, you can't. You gave your word.* Who was I kidding anyway? There was a part of me that wanted to believe him, believe he was telling the truth, believe in him and the words he'd said to me before my trust was shattered.

In the bathroom, when I looked in the mirror, I finally allowed my emotions to take over. I sobbed, because I felt like a fool for letting Jack in when I knew better. I was so desperate to believe him, and look where it had gotten me?

SEVENTEEN

JACK

My head was a mess when I exited Nat's house and got in Dawson's car. The man was very reliable. When I showed up in the lobby early this morning telling him I needed a car, he'd wasted no time in tossing me the keys to his vehicle.

I was tempted to camp out in front of Nat's house and make sure that Maddie wouldn't go back on her word and try to slip out of town. After ten minutes of sitting outside the house in my parked car, I finally admitted that I was being irrational and that stalking her was plain creepy. Plus, if any of Nat's neighbors called the cops on the suspicious dude sitting out in his car, it would not be a good look.

After one more glance at Nat's house, I started the engine and pulled away. I didn't want to go back to the cabin just yet. It felt lonely and empty without her there.

The drive to Austin's house didn't take long at all. I was thankful to see his car out front when I pulled up. I knocked on the door and waited. Seconds later, I could hear footfalls upon his approach. He must have looked out the peephole, because the door wasn't immediately thrown open.

"Listen, I'm sorry for acting like an ass last night."

Austin opened the door but not enough to let me in. "Beg and grovel a little bit more. Maybe one of my neighbors will catch my big, superstar brother on my porch and contact TMZ."

"C'mon. I apologized. I said I was sorry."

Austin rolled his eyes and stepped back to let me enter. When I saw he was still wearing a t-shirt and sweats, I remembered how early it still was.

"I didn't wake you did I?" I walked into his living room and dropped onto the sofa.

"No, I was just about to make myself some breakfast." He headed towards the kitchen but called over his shoulder, "You look like shit by the way."

I could thank the sleepless night I'd had for that. Tossing and turning was about the only thing I did, which was why I'd finally left the house earlier than planned.

After spending a few seconds feeling sorry for myself, I followed Austin into the kitchen. He was already cracking eggs into a skillet. I took a seat at the kitchen table. A plate and some silverware sat in front of one of the chairs.

"So, are you going to tell me why you're here so early and why you needed Maddie's number last night?"

Even though I heard his questions, I sat there staring off into space for a minute. I wasn't looking at my brother when I began to speak. "Everything was going so well. I'd finally gotten her to where she didn't hate me. The day of the reunion we had a good time... Yesterday was probably about one of the most perfect days I'd had in forever that didn't involve my music... until Danielle showed up and blew it all to hell." My voice became bitter at the end. I leaned on the table, scratching at a nick in the surface.

"Danielle, the crazy chick, showed up? How did she know

where you were?" Austin scrambled his eggs while asking the questions.

""Someone sold a picture of me at the resort to a tabloid, and Danielle saw it. Now Maddie thinks I lied to her and that I'm a cheater." I sat back in the chair. "That's why I'm up so early. I went by Nat's house to try and talk to her, but she didn't want to listen to anything I have to say. I think I convinced her to at least stay for the concert."

"Why is it important she stay for the concert?" Austin sounded confused. I looked up at my kid brother.

"Because I have a plan." A little bit of hope filled me when I thought about what I was formulating.

A heavy sigh fell from Austin while he turned off the burner and carried the pan towards the table. Before he made it to the table, he stopped and opened a cabinet, and pulled out another plate. "Bro, I'm all for you trying to win Maddie back..." He sat the extra plate in front of me. "But just remember this concert is to raise money for the foundation. Please don't mess it up." He portioned out the eggs onto both of our plates. When he finished, he placed the pan in the sink and grabbed a fork and handed it to me, before he grabbed a plate of bacon and a stack of toast from the counter and brought it to the table.

I watched him do all of this, but my appetite was lacking. "Sorry... I'm not very hungry."

Austin picked up his fork and pointed at my plate. "Eat up. I doubt you've eaten since all of this went down with Maddie. Plus, you'll need your strength to carry out this plan of yours." He gave me a lopsided grin and then shoveled some eggs into his mouth.

He was right. I hadn't eaten since the late breakfast I made for Maddie and me yesterday. My stomach growled in agreement.

"See," my brother said, indicating he'd heard the loud grumble from my stomach. "Eat."

Reluctantly, I picked up the fork and began to eat.

We'd eaten in complete silence for several minutes before Austin let his fork drop to his plate. He stared at me while he placed an elbow on the table and rested his chin on his closed fist. For a second I kept eating, until I grew uncomfortable and dropped my own fork onto my plate. "What?"

I leaned back in my chair and crossed my arms over my chest.

"I know I didn't tell you that Maddie and I kept in touch after you guys broke up... I've come to care about her like a sister, Jack. She's been there for me at times when you couldn't be..."

Where was he going with this? I leaned forward.

"I know you were miserable for a while when you arrived in Nashville and you were all alone, but I also know the player you turned into. I don't know if you thought you were working Maddie out of your system or what. I just know that if you're really trying to get back with her, just make sure you mean it. Don't play with her. Unlike you, who've not had to watch your ex's life play out in real time: a different woman practically every few months, people reminding her what she missed out on by not going with you... She had to endure that. Why do you think she escaped and never came back here? Too many reminders. So don't break her heart, Jack."

Austin was my brother, but I knew he was implying that he and I would have a problem if I did break Maddie's heart.

Part of me wanted to be angry that my brother would think that I would intentionally hurt her, but I tried to really listen to his words. Looking at my life, and going by appearances, I could see how that would give her pause. I digested my brother's words without saying anything.

He resumed eating his breakfast. I didn't. There was no doubt in my mind that I cared for Maddie, and I wanted her back. I wasn't here to play games or make her another notch on my belt like she'd said. I wanted her plain and simple, and I was willing to do whatever it took to show her that I was serious.

MADDIE

When I emerged from the bathroom after a very long shower, Nat was seated on a barstool in the kitchen, waiting for me with a to-go cup of coffee. She must have gone out or sent Kevin out while I was wallowing in the shower.

Something was different. I looked around the room. It took me a second to realize I didn't hear crying or children's voices or the blare of cartoons, and the room was tidier.

"I had Kevin take them out for a while."

When she handed me the coffee, she offered a small smile. I gave her a sad, but grateful, smile in return and accepted the cup. "Thank you."

Nat wasted no time. "Okay, you've had your shower, and now you have your coffee. Tell me what happened." She took a breath and then plowed on. "You know you can show up on my doorstep at any time. I will always take you in. I'm your friend. What's going on though? Tell me what's up. When you first got here and were forced to share the cabin, I was sure you were going to call me from a jail cell at some point needing bail. Then the two of you left the reunion together like you were Bonnie and Clyde. Today you're throwing coffee cans at his head, and we've come full circle." Nat peered at me with concern. "Okay, I'll shut up now." She took a sip of her coffee and eyed me over the rim.

I chuckled lightly. We sounded like quite the pair when I listened to Natalie's rendition of things.

I ran my finger around the rim of the plastic lid that covered my coffee. "Nat..." I shook my head. My face crumpled. "I should have never given him a second chance to break my heart. His girlfriend showed up after we'd had this beautiful day together." I sniffled.

"She said she was Jack's girlfriend?" Nat raised an eyebrow.

"She didn't have to. He tried to deny it, but I can't trust him." I swallowed down some of the coffee. "Why was I so stupid? I knew better. I'm a freaking lawyer. I had all the evidence right there in those trashy magazines. Why did I let my heart believe that somehow we'd be different? That he'd be different with me?"

She leaned over and rubbed my back. "Don't beat yourself up. It doesn't matter if you were freaking Sherlock Holmes, sweetie, when it comes to matters of the heart, we all do dumb things. You've loved Jack since we were fourteen. He was your first love, your first screw..." We both erupted into laughter when she said that. "And he was your first heartbreak. Yeah we were kids, but you dated for four years. Just because things change doesn't mean the heart just stops caring. Love doesn't work like that. You just got cursed with finding the love of your life at a young age. It was bad timing. I think you and Jack needed to go out into the world and become who you were going to be before you could find your way back to each other."

I wiped at my eyes. "Who said anything about love? I... I... I don't..."

"Oh, honey..." Nat shook her head. "You've got it bad, and you're refusing to admit it. Just say it. You love Jack. Why else would you be all butt hurt over some bimbo that showed up claiming to be his girlfriend if you didn't? I don't know why you're fighting this tooth and nail."

"What?" After everything Nat just said, that was the only thing I could get to come out of my mouth. I'd written closing arguments that could make you weep, and all I could manage was 'What?'

"I think you're looking for a reason not to trust him. You're so afraid of being hurt by him, that you're using this as the excuse to not let yourself be happy."

Natalie was supposed to be my friend. Why was she defending him? My nostrils flared. Agitation churned in my gut. I opened up my mouth to say something, and Natalie held up her hand. "Go to the concert. Hear what he has to say. I mean listen, really listen to him, Maddie. You could be missing out on something good if you don't."

"How did you know he wanted me to stick around for the concert? Were you eavesdropping?"

Nat looked at her watch and drank her coffee. "Uhm, what did you say?"

Her attempt to try and throw me off the fact that she'd listened to part of our conversation made me laugh. I should have known better. Nat had always been nosy. When I let her words sink in, I knew there was some truth to what she said. I didn't want her to be right, but she was.

"Okay... I will listen to what Jack has to say at the concert tomorrow."

"Good. Give the two of you a fair chance... I just want to see you happy Maddie." Nat got down off of her barstool and put her arms around me. I hugged her back.

Once I was alone, I decided I needed to put my lawyer hat on and think about why I would give Jack a second chance. Write out a pros and cons list. This would help me determine what kind of decision I should make.

JACK

After breakfast with Austin, I returned to the cabin. I wasn't sure what to do with myself. Restless and anxious, I prowled the living room like a caged animal. It was weird to be here without her.

How was I going to make Maddie see that I wasn't playing games, that the last thing I wanted to do was hurt her?

I needed to get through the day and keep myself busy. My guitar case was sitting opened on the floor near the sofa. Sheets of paper, along with my notepad, were scattered across the cushions. I had a song to finish. If Maddie kept her word and showed up tomorrow that song was going to show her exactly what she meant to me.

Music had always been a refuge for me to deal with my emotions and feelings, and I needed it to be that now. I sat on the edge of the sofa and picked up my guitar. For a while, I just held the instrument in my hands. My head was in such disarray and my hands shook from my frustration. I couldn't write like this. A few seconds passed, and an inner voice spoke, *just play*.

I took a deep, cleansing breath, and then began to strum

some random notes. The random notes turned into familiar chords, and I realized I was playing "Every Heart Breaks." It was the ballad that Maddie had confessed to be one of her favorites the night she burned her finger.

The trembling in my hands subsided and after minutes of just playing the music, I started singing the lyrics. It gave me a sense of calm I hadn't had since the day Maddie walked out.

After I finished that song, I went on to play and sing another one of my songs. While I did, I thought about Maddie and the last week we'd spent together. Ideas for her song, started to take shape in my mind. Abruptly, I cut myself off in the middle of the chorus and grabbed my notepad and a pencil and furiously started writing. For minutes, I wrote and erased, and then wrote some more, scribbling and crossing out words. After working on a few of the verses, I would pluck out different melodies on my guitar to find something that worked with the words.

Often, I was going back-and-forth between my notepad and playing my guitar as I wrote the song.

In the middle of the afternoon, when my stomach gurgled, I knew I needed to take a break and get some food. Thankfully, there was still some of the groceries that Nat brought over the first day. I wouldn't have to leave the cabin. After eating quickly, I was back at it, plugging away on the song.

Hours later, night had come and gone, the sun was beginning to rise in the sky, but the song was complete. I'd finished Maddie's song, and I was damn proud of it.

I'D STAYED up all night finishing the song. It had been a long time since I'd written a song that had this much meaning to me. I couldn't wait for her to hear it.

The long shower helped revive me, considering I had slept very little. Despite that, I felt energized. Today, I would convince Maddie to give me another shot, and hopefully, it would be the beginning of her putting her faith and trust in me, in us.

Once I dressed, I stood staring into the mirror at my reflection. I sent up a prayer. *Dear God, please let her show up.*

When I left the cabin and headed to the lodge, some other people were on the trail.

"Looking forward to the concert, Jack," someone called out.

I waved and offered a smile I wasn't quite feeling. Rarely, did I get nervous before a concert, but my stomach was in knots wondering if Maddie would be there. I'd always known her to be a woman of her word, but what if she was so hurt, she felt like she didn't need to keep it?

No. She wouldn't do that. Plus, I believed Nat would have tried to let me know if Maddie were planning to leave. I felt like she was secretly rooting for us. I was thankful someone seemed to be in my corner.

Last night, I'd also found myself turning my brother's words over and over again in my head. I would never want to hurt Maddie. I was already sorry I'd ever hurt her to begin with. In my heart, I knew she was the only woman I wanted.

Once I entered through the back of the lodge, I prepared to walk through the lobby but saw Cassie talking to Dawson behind the check-in counter. I walked over to the two of them. "You've both made my stay so pleasant here. I don't know if you're already attending the concert, but wanted to let you know I'm going to leave both of your names at will call, along with a plus one. There will be front row seats waiting for both of you. You'll be my honored guests tonight."

The professionalism that Cassie usually maintained in my

presence went straight out the window. Upon hearing my news, she screeched while jumping up and down, clapping her hands. "Oh my God, my friends are never going to believe this. Thank you. Thank you so much, Mr. Carter."

"Jack."

She blushed. "Sorry, Jack."

Dawson reached out and shook my hand. "Thanks a lot. I'll be there. My sister will be so excited when I tell her. She could use a night off."

Being able to do that for them made me feel good. I headed outside and found the car service waiting to take me to the theater where the benefit concert was to be held.

Knowing I was headed into sound check and rehearsal, and that my band had flown in for this as a favor to me, made me set my personal issues to the side. I had a show to put on. On the drive, I cleared my mind and started going through the set list in my head. I was still using Maddie's choices, in the order she'd suggested them in.

At the theater, I found my band already on stage warming up. I was happy to see those guys.

"Hey Jack," a familiar voice called out, and I was surprised to find Janine, entering from the side of the stage.

"Thought you weren't going to come." I walked up the steps to the stage, wearing a genuine smile.

"I figured you probably needed me so I hitched a ride with these guys." I gave her a hug, which she acted like she didn't like, but like I said she's a big softy.

"So what songs did you decide on?" Mel asked. He was already seated at his drums.

Over the next couple hours, while we went through the set list, I was able to focus. Maddie and whether she'd show up tonight only crept into my mind a few times.

Once we decided we had enough rehearsal time, everyone left the stage and went to their dressing rooms. I motioned for Janine to follow me. "Can you post someone outside to wait for someone?"

"Jack, you do realize nearly the whole town is coming to this thing? How is someone supposed to find one person?"

I pulled my phone out and showed her a picture of Maddie I'd pulled off of the law firm's website she worked at. "Give them this photo. Tell them once she arrives to bring her to one of the front row seats I had them rope off, okay?" I texted the photo to Janine. "It's important."

She was about to say something sarcastic, but when she looked in my face, she must have seen that this wasn't some groupie or just any woman. Janine swallowed down her snarky comment and grew serious. "Okay. I'll make sure I have a designated person to look out for her and that they bring her to sit in the front row."

While she went to deal with that, I went to my dressing room and put on a different shirt. Under the glare of the spotlights, it got hot pretty quickly, and after our rehearsal I needed to change shirts. I checked my phone to see if I had any missed calls or texts. It was wishful thinking. I knew Maddie wasn't going to call. Either she was going to show up or she wouldn't.

Twenty minutes later, someone knocked on the door.

"Come in," I shouted.

My brother stepped into the room. "Just wanted to see how you're doing."

"How's the crowd out there?"

"People are so pumped for this concert. I can't thank you enough for doing this. We're going to raise a lot of money tonight." Austin was so grateful.

"It's for the kids, right?" I grinned.

"Yeah... for the kids." I could tell my brother wanted to say more.

Neither of us said anything for a minute.

"About..." Austin began, but I cut him off.

"You don't have to. You were being a good friend to her. She's lucky to have you in her corner... I don't think I ever stopped loving her, Austin. I didn't use to believe that you could fall in love with someone at such a young age. When I got here that day and saw Maddie in the lobby, it was..." I sighed.

"I started to understand why I never grew serious with any of those other women. They weren't Maddie. I was just too young and dumb to know that then, but I think my heart has always known. I love her, and I promise you... I won't hurt her."

"Good, because I might not play football anymore, but believe I could still kick your ass if you do."

I doubled over in a belly laugh. Although I laughed, there was probably a good possibility that Austin could kick my ass. He wasn't my little kid brother anymore.

My brother walked over and gave me a bear hug.

"Now get out so I can get ready for the concert," I chuckled.

Austin patted me on the back and left.

We had another thirty minutes before the show started. I sat on the sofa. My palms were clammy because I was nervous Maddie would be a no-show. I wiped them off on my jeans.

In the mirror, I looked at my reflection and reminded myself that even if she chose not to show up here tonight, that it wasn't the end. If I had to go to New York and find her, I would.

More time ticked by, and someone wrapped on the door.

"Showtime," I said to myself.

When I left the dressing room and followed the stage manager to the place backstage I would enter from, I still held out hope that she would show. Janine hadn't called or sent word that she'd arrived, so I knew when I got out there I was going to find an empty seat.

Currently, Austin was out on stage, talking about the foundation that the proceeds from the ticket sales would benefit and thanking everyone for opening up their wallets.

One of the sound guys fitted me for my earpiece and microphone while I listened. I strapped on my guitar, knowing Austin would introduce me soon. As my band passed me, they each patted me on the shoulder before they headed onto the stage. The rumble of applause as each of them took their position made me smile.

"And now, my big brother, Jack Carter," my brother roared.

The band had already started to play the chords for "Let's Party Every Night." The crowd was on their feet and going wild when I walked out onstage. I tried to avoid looking at the empty seat in the front row that was meant for her. Waving to the crowd, I took my place center stage.

"How are y'all doing tonight?" I amped up the country charm, and grinned, knowing I had to deliver. These people had paid good money to see me.

One of the pitfalls of being a performer was sometimes you had to perform, even when your heart was breaking. You had to put on a smile and pretend like everything was right with the world.

"Y'all ready for this?"

People whooped and cheered. A couple rows back, some of the clowns from the reunion applauded and whistled. Nat and Kevin were seated in the second row. They waved to me. Christopher Richards was a few seats over and grinned up at the stage like a fool. He'd probably told all of his buddies we were best friends. He struck me as the type.

When I finally did let myself glance at the front row, I saw Dawson with his sister, and Cassie had one of her friends with her. Both of them were squealing so loudly, I was afraid their heads would pop off. I grinned and waved to her. If possible, she screamed even louder.

Strumming the well-known chords to the party anthem that everyone seemed to love, I began to sing. The theater maybe held a thousand people, but for all the noise they made we could have been playing to a stadium full of people. Those that didn't get to their feet when I initially walked on stage, jumped up the minute we hit the first chorus. Midway through the song, the other guitarist and I dueled back and forth, amping the crowd up even more as we riffed. I went back to the microphone for the last half. Wanting to do a little call and response, I flipped my guitar around until it was behind me and pulled the microphone from the stand and held it out to the audience. They sang the song perfectly. When we came to the end, I put the microphone back on the stand and finished the song.

They clapped and cheered so loudly that I had to quiet them down, before we went on to the next song. The band had already begun to play the next song when I looked down and saw an usher guiding Maddie to her seat. She wasn't looking at me. Her hair wasn't straight like it had been all week. She wore it like she'd done in high school. Her natural curls fell in ringlets framing her face. The skinny jeans she wore accentuated her curves, and the tight cardigan sweater showed off her perky breasts.

My heart flipped over in my chest. I was so grateful she was there. The cue for me to come into the song had just happened, but my eyes were still locked on her. Mel and my bassist played the chords again.

Maddie finally looked up at me. Her expression was unreadable. I held up my hand for the band to stop. I hadn't shared the plan with my bandmates during the rehearsal. The song was still so new right now, the arrangement only suited my voice and the guitar since I hadn't written in a studio where I could fool around and write more instruments into the arrangement.

The place was pin-drop quiet while everyone waited to see why I halted the show. My gaze was locked on her when I began to speak. "Many of you know I grew up here. PA boy, born and bred." Some catcalled from the audience.

"What some of you may not know is that I met and fell in love with the prettiest little firecracker in the world my freshman year of high school, and we dated for those four years... a pair of misfits." My heart was so full of love for this woman.

"I never told her that she was my first too. Being older, I'm not embarrassed to admit that." There was some laughter and snickering in the crowd.

Maddie slumped in her seat, and covered her face with her hand, but I could see that smile of hers that lit up my heart. She peered at me through her fingers.

"I broke her heart when I left here, which I will forever be sorry for. More importantly, I'm sorry that I didn't always see her, what she needed, what she wanted. I was too young, dumb, and immature to appreciate what I had. Take notes, men." A lot of people in the crowd laughed at that one. I even saw some girlfriends and wives elbowing boyfriends and spouses in the sides. Grinning, I turned my focus back to Maddie.

"I'm laying it all out there. Laying myself bare, because I need her to know she has my heart, and she always has. Maddie Grace... you are my first and only love. This song is for you. It's called 'Stuck With You.'"

Some of the women in the audience sighed.

I began to pluck and strum the notes on my guitar before I started singing the lyrics to the song that had taken shape that day in my head at the bar.

Slowly, Maddie's hand slipped from her face, the more I

sang, and the more of the lyrics she heard, until her hand was in her lap. She sat up straighter, and I was pretty sure I saw a tear slip down her cheek.

When I finally finished, everyone stood and clapped their hands and yelled their appreciation for the song. Some people sitting near Maddie touched her shoulder or said things to her, which I couldn't hear. I wished it was the end of the show and I could go to her, but our reconciliation would have to wait until after the show.

"Okay, ladies and gentleman, thank you for indulging me, and now we resume with our regularly scheduled program." Laughter rippled throughout the audience. When the band played the chords for "Every Girl's A Tease," this time I came in on cue.

During this song, all the ladies were on their feet, singing all the lyrics, shimmying, and doing a bunch of dance moves. Maddie was definitely right. I saw some men in the audience that looked like they might get laid off their lady hearing that one song tonight. It seemed to bring out their inner stripper. My gaze landed on Maddie. She was singing along, just like all the other women and shaking those sexy hips with the beat. I wondered if this song brought out her inner stripper. I hoped I'd get the opportunity to find out.

We finished out the night to the sounds of everyone yelling for an encore, so I pulled another song out of my hat, and we performed a final number.

Thank God Janine was such a great assistant; before I exited the stage, I could see that she'd already sent an usher to bring Maddie backstage. Usually, I waited to walk off stage with the band, but I was in such a rush to get to Maddie.

"Slow down, or you're gonna hurt yourself, man." Mel chuckled and unhooked my guitar strap that had gotten caught on something in my haste to get to Maddie. He unhooked it with a chuckle.

I took the towel the roadie offered me and wiped down my face and neck. Yeah, I was still a sweaty mess, but at least I wouldn't be a shiny sweaty mess. I jogged to the entrance that I knew they'd have to enter through, and I waited.

TWENTY

MADDIE

So many thoughts were going through my mind as I followed Jack's assistant, Janine, backstage. Even after Jack's grand gesture, a tiny part of me still questioned if I was doing the right thing. My pros and cons list flitted through my head.

People we passed along the way gave me knowing glances and smiles. A group of girls even shouted, "Yay, Maddie," at me like I'd done something that deserved recognition, besides be serenaded. I was a little unnerved by all the attention and kept my head down to avoid making eye contact.

Janine looked at me out of the corner of her eye. "So you're the one that has Jack ready to jump on sofas like Tom Cruise."

The smirk that followed her comment made me giggle. I could see why Jack liked having her around. "The one and only, apparently."

"I think I'm going to like you much better than Danielle the dingbat. At least that's what I called her." She shook her head and rolled her eyes. "She's trash. I was so happy when he kicked her ass to the curb like a month ago."

I almost told Janine I wasn't sure if I was sticking around, but I was focused on the fact that she'd mentioned Jack broke up with Danielle weeks ago. Janine didn't strike me as the type to lie for her boss, plus I didn't think Jack shared details about his relationships with her, which meant that Jack was telling the truth.

Despite knowing the truth, I didn't plan to make it easy for him. I wasn't just going to rush into his arms.

When we walked through the double doors leading to back-stage, I wasn't prepared to find Jack waiting there. People milled about with cables and instruments, talking on walkie-talkies and doing their jobs. Janine melted into the crowd without another word and left Jack and me alone. Well, as alone as you could be in a busy hallway.

I was still about ten feet away from him. He didn't try to approach. I eyed him, still unsure what I was going to say. I thought I had more time. Jack looked ruggedly handsome, like he'd just been baling hay after a long day instead of singing. The tight-fitting t-shirt he wore was wet from all the sweating, but it showed off his well-defined pecs, biceps and abs. That stubble though, it's what got me every time.

Who was I kidding? If he wanted me, there was no way I was letting him go. But I had to play it cool, make him think I was still angry.

"If you think that just by singing a song that you're going to win me back..." I walked towards Jack, doing by best to suppress the smile that kept trying to spread across my face. He saw right through me.

"What about the huge public apology I just made on stage? I humiliated myself. Doesn't that count for anything?" He faked incredulity as he walked towards me.

A short distance away from him, I stopped and held up two fingers a few inches apart and scrunched up my nose. "Just a little bit."

When he closed the distance between us, I peered into his

eyes.

"Do you forgive me?" The humor was wiped from his face.

The vindictive part of me wanted to make him sweat. I looked away and bit my lip like I was contemplating my answer. Then I looked at him. "Yes."

When Jack whooped with joy, picked me up in his arms, and twirled me around, I couldn't stop my giggles, or the broad grin I wore either. He sat my feet back on the ground and cupped my face in his hands. The way those gray-blue eyes stared into mine took my breath away.

"I don't care if you think it's too soon, but I love you, Maddie girl. You have my whole heart." When he pressed his lips to mine, I closed my eyes, wrapped my arms around him, and lost myself in the best kiss ever. I'm sure there were probably some epic kisses in our future, but to date this one topped them all.

It didn't matter if we had an audience at this point. It just felt good to be back in Jack's arms.

LATER THAT NIGHT, we lay on our bellies at the foot of the bed, watching TV. Earlier we'd had a marathon round of sex that started in the living room before we finally made it to his bedroom. I had on one of Jack's t-shirts, but he'd refused to put on any clothes. We were eating ice cream out of the carton. The reality show we were watching had just gone to commercial when Jack turned to me.

"When you showed up late to the concert..."

I snickered at him bringing up me being late to the concert and licked ice cream off my spoon. I noticed his gaze following the actions of my mouth. "Are you really going to go there?"

He chuckled, and his gaze darted back up to my eyes. "I just want to know if it was intentional. Were you trying to make me sweat?"

In all honesty, I'd arrived to the theater ahead of the show, but fear had kept me from making it inside on time. I'd pulled out my pros and cons list to reassure myself I was making the right decision before I headed inside.

I dropped my spoon into the nearly empty carton and propped myself on my elbow. For long seconds I stared at him. "Truthfully, it wasn't intentional. I was looking at the pros and cons list I made about whether I should forgive you or not."

That really got his attention. "You made a pros and cons list? Can I see it?"

"No, you may not. It was for my eyes only."

He poked out his lip and pouted. "C'mon. Please." His hands started roaming over my hips, pushing up his t-shirt I was wearing. I grinned and pushed his hands away. We both knew I wasn't wearing any panties.

"No." I giggled.

"Please, Maddie girl." His voice was so low and husky, it had me squeezing my legs together. He kissed my collarbone.

"Jack you're not playing fair."

"I never said I would..." He kissed my breast through the thin cotton shirt and then looked up at me with this predatory look. "Let me see the list?"

He was going to keep it up until he had me right where he wanted me: so hot and bothered, and on the verge of a climax that he would snatch away until I showed him the list.

His fingers trailed up the inside of my thigh, on the way to the slick heat between my legs. "Okay, okay... you fight dirty."

He kissed me and moved his hand to rest on my hip. "I know, and you love it." He gave me a smirk.

"Would you settle for me sharing a few things that were on the list with you?"

Jack narrowed his eyes in suspicion, trying to figure out if I was gaming him. His hard dick brushed my thigh, and I shivered.

"I promise, it will be the truth." I wet my lip with my tongue.

The reality show had come back from commercial break, but neither of us cared.

"One of the pros on my list was that you bring out the kid in me, the fun side. I'm not so uptight."

That made him grin, exposing those blindingly white teeth of his. "Inner tubing down the slope. Maybe we could sneak out there tomorrow night?"

I nodded.

"Okay, what was one of the cons on your list?" He brushed a strand of hair away from my face.

Without hesitating I said the first con that made my list. "You make me crazy."

"You love it when I make you crazy, and you know I love you all feisty. I think that should be on your pro list." Jack leaned in and kissed me deeply. When he pulled away, he pressed his lips to my forehead. "What's another pro?"

After his kiss and the fact that he was now massaging my hip, I wasn't concentrating. "Hmm?"

"What's your next pro?"

"Oh... we always have a good time when we're together." I smiled lazily at him.

He chuckled. "I don't think you had that much fun when I dragged you out to do ice fishing."

"I had fun, because I was with you, especially when I got to snuggle in your lap."

"You liked that?"

I nodded. "Yeah. I didn't even mind you being bossy... it kind of turned me on."

"Oh yeah?" His voice had gone husky again.

I nodded.

"What's another con?"

I didn't want to give him another con, because the pros had outweighed the cons. So I gave him the top reason that I walked into the concert. I shook my head. "No... no more cons."

Jack was ready to say something, but I pressed a finger to his lips to stop him. "I want to tell you the biggest pro that trumps all the cons." I took my finger away from his mouth. "I love you. I've always loved you. Even when I thought I hated you, I didn't. You said you loved me earlier today, and I appreciate you not being upset that I didn't say it right after you said it..." Okay, now I was rambling.

Jack sat the ice cream carton on the ground. Without saying anything, he grabbed the remote and turned off the TV. He tossed the remote onto the floor, where it landed on some of our clothes. His gaze raked my face, and he pulled his t-shirt over my head, so I was just as naked as he was.

While he stared at my body, his hands roamed everywhere turning me into a puddle of need. My thighs fell open, tempting him, inviting him. He slid two fingers inside me. I moaned when he pushed them in deeper and pulled them out, pushed them in, then pulled them out.

A few seconds later, he removed his fingers and sucked them clean, before he rocked back on his heels and grabbed a condom from the dresser. I watched with anticipation as he tore the wrapper open and slid the condom onto his dick. When he positioned himself between my legs and thrust into me, I welcomed it. He buried his face in my neck, kissing and licking, while delivering drugging strokes to my core.

He made love to me all night long. By the time we were both

sated, the sun was climbing the sky. I was slipping into unconsciousness when Jack whispered in my ear. "I love you, Maddie girl. You're stuck with me."

EPILOGUE

JACK

One Year Later...

"GOOD EVENING NEW YORK CITY," I yelled over the crowd in Madison Square Garden. The room erupted in celebration, and I ate up their adoration. Concerts always made me feel like I was on top of the world.

"Thank you for welcoming me with open arms to your wonderful city. I'll miss Nashville, but you're my new home now since my lady lives here." I looked off stage, and Maddie waved at me from the wings. My woman was so damn beautiful that she took my breath away.

"Y'all, we're going to kick it off with my recent, Grammy-winning number one new single that's topping the charts, 'Stuck With You.' That all right with you guys?"

More cheering.

"You know what? Why don't we get my wife out here? I wrote the song for her. What do you guys think?"

The audience clapped and stomped their approval.

"Maddie girl, I think you better bring your lovely ass out here." I motioned for her to join me on stage.

Maddie shook her head and mouthed an emphatic no. One of the cameras swung in her direction to catch her. She looked mortified and tried to hide her face. Austin, who was standing behind her, gave her a slight push until she was out on the stage. The crowd applauded her while she made a slow, nervous trek across the stage to reach my side. I put my arm around her and drew her closer.

"I'm going to kill you for this," she mumbled, but she smiled and waved to the crowd. I kissed her forehead and chuckled.

One of the production assistants brought out a stool for Maddie to sit on. I took her hand and helped her up onto the stool. The band began to play the song. Some of the arrangement had changed slightly since my first performance of it at the benefit concert in the Poconos, but it was still a ballad.

The minute I started singing, many of the people in the crowd held up some kind of light. It was a mixture of cell phones and glow sticks. Everyone swayed to the beat. I could see it all in my periphery, but my gaze was glued to Maddie.

Midway through the song, I flipped my guitar around so it lay against my back, and to her surprise I got down on my knees. I caressed Maddie's belly, and sung the lyrics to the baby that was growing in her womb. We'd just found out that morning that we were going to be parents, and she'd agreed I could share the news tonight. She just hadn't known I was planning to make her a part of it.

When Maddie placed her hand over the top of mine, I looked up at her face. She was misty-eyed. I could hear the gasps of excitement from the audience when everyone realized we were pregnant. Someone yelled out "Congratulations," while I was finishing the final lyric.

I rose to my feet when the band played the final notes, pulled Maddie from the stool, and kissed her with abandon, in front of the crowd. When I pulled away, she licked her bottom lip.

"Give it up for my baby mama, everyone."

That made Maddie giggle, like I knew it would. Playfully, she smacked my arm. "Okay, baby daddy."

I swatted her on that luscious ass of hers when she left the stage. As she walked away, my gaze was locked on the sway of her hips, before launching into the next song. "Who's ready to party every night? Make some noise!"

The crowd went wild, and the band started up the party anthem that always got the crowd off their feet. Now that they'd had a little bit of sweet, I planned to keep them rocking out for a while before I sang another ballad again.

AFTER THE CONCERT, we were on our way to the airport. Today was the one-year anniversary from when we reunited, and I was surprising her with a trip.

Our second chance love story had been a bit of a whirlwind. We started dating after the benefit concert, and I proposed six months later. When she made partner at her law firm in New York, I was so damn proud of her. I wanted her to know I wasn't that teenage kid anymore, the one that had been selfishly focused on his own career that I forgot about hers. Just like she often sat in the front row of my concerts or stood in the wings cheering me on, I wanted to show her that I was her biggest cheerleader, believer, and supporter, so I moved to New York.

Within a month, we were married in a small ceremony that only included our families and closest friends. Neither of us wanted anything big. Our life was already a bit of a spectacle because I was famous. We wanted that moment to be just for us.

Maddie made a noise in her sleep, breaking me from my introspective mood. She was curled up next to me in the back of the SUV sleeping.

I placed my hand on her stomach. We would be parents soon. I couldn't wait to raise a family, with my Maddie girl. She was going to make a great mother.

When we arrived at the airport, my private jet was waiting. I didn't want to wake her, so I carried her from the car and onto the plane and laid her in the bedroom before we took off. The pregnancy had her so tired lately.

She'd been asking me for weeks where I was taking her. It was fun letting her guess. I guess with all the grandiose gestures I'd done over time, she assumed it would be some exotic location. I couldn't wait to see her face.

While she slept on the flight, I phoned ahead and made sure that all the arrangements had been taken care of. Once those calls were completed, I checked some emails. It was hard not to be a little excited. We'd both been so busy lately. This would be the first time in about a month when we weren't fitting each other in between work. It would just be the two of us.

About forty minutes later, the plane landed. I went into the bedroom to wake Maddie up.

"Maddie girl, wake up. We're here." I sat on the side of the bed and stroked her back.

"We're here?" Her eyes were still closed.

Looking at her, adorably groggy from sleep, I suddenly hoped we had a little girl that looked like her.

Finally, she sat up and rubbed the sleep from her eyes. She leaned over and kissed my cheek. "Are you going to tell me yet where we are?" She stretched her arms above her head and yawned.

I shook my head. "Nope. Also, I'm going to need to blind-fold you before you get off the plane."

She smiled. "You and your surprises."

I knew she secretly loved them.

"Okay. I'll wear the blindfold."

I took her hands and helped her up from the bed. She turned so she was facing away from me, making it easier for me to apply the blindfold.

We walked out into the main cabin, and I draped her coat over her shoulders and helped her disembark. In the back of the SUV, she leaned on me.

"I can't wait to see where you decided on." She whispered.

"I can't wait for you to see either." I whispered back.

When we drove down the familiar driveway I took her hand in mine. About ten minutes later, the car came to a stop.

"We're here."

I helped her out of the car and let the driver put our luggage inside before I took her blindfold off.

"Thank you." I handed him a tip, even though I was pretty sure Janine would have included one when she booked the reservation. Once he pulled away and we were alone, I pulled off her blindfold. "Surprise."

Maddie began to giggle when she saw cabin fifty-three, the cabin we'd stayed in at Holiday Springs Resort, a year ago.

"I thought it only fitting that we come stay here to celebrate the anniversary of our reunion."

Her eyes sparkled. "I love it." She wrapped her arms around my neck and kissed me.

We walked up the steps together and headed inside. A fire was already roaring in the fireplace, and Dawson already had everything I requested waiting in the cabin.

I had plans to make up for the s'mores debacle. Plus, we were going to have our night of passion in front of that fireplace, with oysters, chocolate-covered strawberries, the whole seduction. As far as I was concerned, I would be turning off our phones and hiding them. If she brought any case files from work, I planned to hide those too. This next week was just about us. I planned to keep her naked all week long.

I noticed that Dawson had even gone through the trouble of them laying out the blankets and pillows before the fireplace.

Maddie smiled up at me. "I'm so glad you chose this place. I was hoping you would pick here."

"Why didn't you say anything?"

"Because I wanted to see if you'd choose it on your own. And you did."

I shut the front door and helped her take off her jacket.

"I'm going to go freshen up and make myself comfortable." She grabbed the handle of her bag and wheeled it toward the bedrooms. "Which room do you want?"

When she turned around and looked at me, I stared back at her like she'd lost her mind. "What do you mean, which room do I want? You're my wife."

Maddie doubled over in laughter. "Gotcha."

I chased after her, and we ended up freshening up in the shower together before we made it back out to the living room to enjoy the fire.

Hours later, after making love in front of the fire, we lay together sated. My hand was slowly rubbing circles over her belly.

"I'm so happy, Jack."

I looked down at her.

"Lying here with you right now and expecting our first child together, it reminded me of last year when we were here, and how you told me there was something missing from your life. I hadn't wanted to admit it then, but you were right." She laid her hand over mine on her stomach.

"I'm really happy too, Maddie Girl. There's nowhere else I'd rather be than right here with you." I kissed the side of her head and snuggled her into my body. Life would never be sweeter than it was right now.

SECOND START - BOOK #5

Next from the Holiday Springs Series
Second Start by S.E. Rose
Holiday Springs, Book #5
Releasing 11/20/2020

Will a former Olympic athlete and budding musician get a second chance at their happily ever after?

Brittany Evans and Tyson Mitchell were the "it" couple in the Poconos. Until their own dreams and goals got in the way. With broken hearts, they both left their town while doing their best to never look back.

But, when a skiing injury and a failed singing career bring them both back home, they find that their feelings may not have iced over after all.

Fate has brought them together again, but if Tyson wants to win back Brittany's heart, he'll have to prove that she's the only dream that matters.

Escape to the romantic paradise of Holiday Springs and warm-up with your next happily ever after, in Second Start.

Visit https://www.facebook.com/HolidaySpringsSeries for all the details.

HOLIDAYS SPRINGS SERIES LIST

Nestled deep in the mountains of Pennsylvania, Holiday Springs Resort promises to bring the heat this winter! Seven amazing authors as they take to the slopes on the adventure of a lifetime and find their happily ever afters. For more information, visit the series website:
https://www.facebook.com/HolidaySpringsSeries/

It's Always Been You by A.M. Williams
A Friends to Lovers Romance

Deal Breaker by Julie Archer
A Best Friend's Sibling Romance

Love on the Rocks by Kim Bailey
A Workplace Romance

Stuck With You by Moni Boyce
An Enemies to Lovers Romance

Second Start by S.E. Rose

A Second Chance Romance

Love Rebooted by Stacey Lewis
A Widower Romance

Something New by B. Ivy Woods
A Jilted Bride Romance

ALSO BY MONI BOYCE

Contemporary Romance:

Redemption of the Heart (standalone)

Love Delayed In Dublin: Ticket to True Love

All I Want For Christmas Is An Alpha: A Very Alpha Christmas
Season 2, Book 3

Paranormal Romance:

Awakened: The Oracle Chronicles Book 1

Enlightened: The Oracle Chronicles Book 2

Empowered: The Oracle Chronicles Book 3

Divined: The Oracle Chronicles Book 4

Anthologies:

Big City Heat Romance Anthology

STAY CONNECTED

Website: https://moniboyce.com
Amazon: https://www.amazon.com/author/moniboyce
Bookbub: https://www.bookbub.com/authors/moni-boyce
FB Group: https://www.facebook.com/groups/monismob
Goodreads: https://www.goodreads.com/moniboyce
Facebook: https://www.facebook.com/MoniBoyceWrites
Twitter: https://www.twitter.com/moniboyce
Instagram: https://www.instagram.com/moniboyce
Pinterest: https://www.pinterest.com/moniboyce
Book + Main Bites: https://www.
bookandmainbites.com/moniboyce
Radish: https://radishfiction.com/users/MoniBoyce
**To join newsletter, click on banner at the top of the page on
my website.

ACKNOWLEDGMENTS

First and foremost, I always acknowledge and thank God for being able to do what I love. Without Him, none of this would be possible. Thanks to Lauren and Aubree for inviting me to be part of this amazingly talented bunch of writers. I enjoyed writing in the world of Holiday Springs. It was a lot of fun creating and writing Jack and Maddie and watching them find their way back to each other. A special thanks to the awesome editors, proofreaders and beta readers that helped polish the story. Thanks to Kim for the awesome cover. I'm always super appreciative of the incredible support and encouragement I receive from my family and friends. A huge thank you and I love you to each of you. A huge shout out to all the awesome readers that read this book. I hope you enjoyed it. I'm tremendously grateful for all of you, for the new readers that may be reading my work for the first time, and for the loyal fans that pick up my books time and again. Thank you.

PLEASE LEAVE A REVIEW

If you enjoyed the book, please share this book with family

and friends, post about it on social media, or consider leaving a review. I would be extremely grateful.

ABOUT THE AUTHOR

Moni Boyce is an award-winning author of contemporary and paranormal romance, a filmmaker and a poet. After working in the film industry for fifteen years, helping others bring their visions to life, she now creates characters and worlds of her own. She considers herself a bookworm, film buff, foodie, music lover and an avid world traveler having visited 33 countries and counting. She currently lives in Virginia but considers Los Angeles her hometown.